THE COWBOY'S HOME

DIXON RANCH SERIES - BOOK ONE

CHRISTINA BUTRUM

Copyright © 2021 by CHRISTINA Butrum

All rights reserved.

No part of this book may be reproduced in any form or by any electronic or mechanical means, including information storage and retrieval systems, without written permission from the author, except for the use of brief quotations in a book review.

Edited by: Three Owls Editing

Cover by: Daniel at thebookbrander.com

Formatted by: Christina Butrum

"It's a funny thing coming home. Nothing changes. Everything looks the same, feels the same, even smells the same. You realize what's changed is you."

F. Scott Fitzgerald

CHAPTER ONE

The accident had nearly cost him his life. Thankfully, he still had it. What he didn't have, though, was the courage he needed to face his brother.

Drew Dixon pulled into the driveway and parked near the main house. He debated on whether or not to kill the engine or to keep his old truck running for a quick getaway before settling on the latter and stepping out.

The moment his cowboy boots touched the gravel, he felt the surge of being home run through him. Aside from the mix of torment and regret, it felt good to be standing on familiar ground. There was nothing better than the wide-open spaces of Montana.

"What are you doing here?"

Drew tore his attention away from the pastel-colored sky and focused on the man asking him the million-dollar question. The question he'd been dreading since deciding to make his way back home.

"Nice to see you, too," he said sarcastically, refusing to answer his brother's question. Blake, of all people, should've known why he was there. His brother had told him time and again the rodeo wasn't good for anything, and he'd be lucky if a bull didn't stomp right through him when given the chance. With his left arm held up in a sling, it should've been obvious to Blake that Drew cashed in on some of that luck.

"This isn't the time for pleasantries," Blake scolded, standing guard of the property. Confusion knit tightly in Blake's brow as he gave Drew a once-over, narrowing his focus on the slung arm.

Standing in awkward silence, Drew glanced at the duffle bag sitting on the bench seat of his truck and wondered why he'd thought coming back home was a good idea. The duffle bag, his truck, and the ranch were the only things he had left in his name. The rodeo, along with a year of bad choices, hadn't left him with much else.

"From the looks of it," his brother started, motioning between the sling on Drew's arm to the duffle bag, "things didn't go as planned with the rodeo?"

"I guess you could say that," Drew said, allowing

the jab to roll off his back. He wouldn't add fuel to the fire the two of them had started last year. The flames had gotten out of control, and if Drew were to be honest, he regretted fighting with Blake. "Three seconds from beating the clock, and all I got out of it was a torn rotator cuff. The doc says it could take a while to heal."

Drew could tell Blake wasn't listening to a word he was saying. His brother couldn't care less about the rodeo and the injuries Drew received. Losing their father to the rodeo didn't help, and with Blake being the oldest of the three Dixon brothers, he had taken it upon himself to make sure Garrett and Drew stayed on the straight and narrow.

"Says it could take up to six months," Drew explained anyway, "possibly longer. I kinda zoned out when he started talking about the healing process and how long it will take to get back to the rodeo."

Blake furrowed his brow and shook his head. "You're never going to learn, are you?"

Drew remained quiet, unsure if Blake's question demanded an answer.

"So, what's your plan?" Blake asked, pushing off the front end of the truck and taking a few steps toward Drew. Drew stayed quiet, knowing his brother didn't really want an answer. Instead, Blake wanted to do what he did best—lecture. He would lecture Drew about the risks and worthlessness of the rodeo until he was blue in the face and couldn't stand talking anymore. He'd swear he was talking to a brick wall before stomping off toward the main house. Drew knew his brother all too well, and just like clockwork, the lecture started. "You know you should've thought twice about it before leaving."

Drew shut the door and leaned against it, hesitant to say a word knowing where the conversation would end up. He hadn't wanted to leave the ranch last year. He'd wanted to run it right alongside Blake and Garrett, but once their uncle, Curt, moved to Maple Glen, everything flipped on a dime and the ownership went straight to Blake's head.

"The rodeo isn't good business," Blake said. "Pops thought the same way you do now, and look where it got—"

"Don't bring him into this," Drew said through gritted teeth at the mention of their father, a man neither one of them really got to know. "This has nothing to do with him."

Blake narrowed his eyes on him, and Drew felt the heat coming from the glare. Pushing away from the truck, Drew held up his hands in defense and said, "Look, I didn't come back here to start an argument."

Blake let out a loud grunt as he tipped his hat. "Could've fooled me."

Drew hadn't thought too far ahead after his arrival at the ranch, but arguing with Blake hadn't been on the agenda. He wanted to arrive, make amends, and carry on with life the way it had been before he'd left town. He could understand why that would be a hard pill for Blake to swallow. Drew hadn't left on good terms, and at the time he hadn't cared enough to turn back and make things right.

"One of these days you're going to learn what life's all about," Blake said, "and hopefully you'll figure it out before it's too late."

Drew shook his head in silent objection. "Like you've got it all figured out, huh?"

"I've got a lot more going for me than you ever will," Blake growled, taking a step toward Drew. Drew kept his stance, refusing to back down. His brother's words stung, but Drew wouldn't give him the satisfaction he was looking for.

"You wouldn't have anything if it wasn't for Curt," Drew retorted, keeping his emotions in check. He'd like to think he matured over the last year, but at the moment, that theory was being tested. "You know darn well this ranch would've been long gone the day Pops died if it'd been up to Ma."

The words flew out of his mouth without a second thought. By the troubled look on Blake's face, his words had struck a nerve. Drew had only spoken the truth. He'd just been a little boy the day their father had died in a rodeo accident, but he'd heard their uncle talk about things from time to time. If it hadn't been for Curt moving to Montana, and taking over the ranch, none of the Dixon brothers would have a dime to fight over. Mama Dixon would have sold it without so much as a second thought. Thankfully, Curt had talked her out of selling the ranch and moving out of state. Somehow he'd convinced her to stay put and let him take care of everything that needed taken care of. The Dixon brothers wouldn't have been raised on the ranch their father had started if it hadn't been for their uncle.

"Listen," Drew said, looking down as he kicked loose gravel with the toe of his boot. "I can't tell you what I was thinking when I left last year, and even if I could, you'd still see it as an excuse—"

"Cut the pity," Blake scolded, dropping his arms at his side and taking a step toward Drew. "Just face it. Things didn't go the way you'd hoped they would out in the real world, and now you're back with an injured arm and your bruised pride."

Drew took the jabs and allowed Blake's words to roll off. There was no sense in making things worse when his priority was to make amends. He wanted a place to call home, along with somewhere he didn't have to worry about his next meal. He'd lost a lot of money in the city while participating in bull riding competitions. No matter if he was making money or not, he still spent it. He'd blown through his savings in record time at the local casinos and bars.

"How long are you planning to stay this time around?"

Blake's question required an honest answer, but Drew wasn't too sure he could give him one. Sure, he'd planned to stick around for the time being, waiting out the healing of his shoulder, but at the end of the day, he knew once it was healed, he would be on his way to the next rodeo competition he could find.

"So we're just a pit stop, huh?" Blake asked, kicking gravel and shaking his head in disbelief. "Just a place to collect your things, save up some money, and heal before chasing your next eight-second ride?"

Drew stayed quiet. Blake knew him better than anyone, and to say his brother had hit the nail on the head would have been an understatement.

Blake removed his cowboy hat and ran a hand through his sweat-matted hair. Drew could see the lines of frustration crease in his brother's forehead but wasn't too sure he knew what to say to make him relax. Life for Blake wasn't the same as it was for Drew. The two of them had never really seen eye to eye, and it had only been because of Curt the two of them had gotten along for as long as they had.

Drew had thought about his uncle from time to time while traveling from one circuit to the next. Most of the time, it had been a passing thought, wondering what Uncle Curt would do if he were in

Drew's shoes. Of course, Drew knew exactly what Curt would have done, and it was far from what would have been expected of Drew.

"You know there's more to life than the rodeo, right?" Blake asked, pulling Drew out of his thoughts and making him refocus. "There's the ranch, for one. A ranch that our own father started from the ground up. One that our uncle poured hours of blood, sweat, and tears into just to make sure we had a place to live and were comfortable."

Drew bit back the comment he wanted to make in reference to their dead father and shook his head. He'd thought about their father more in the last year than he had in the rest of his entire thirty-two years. He'd thought about what life would've been like if they'd had their father to raise them, and how different things would've been had he not died in a rodeo accident. Of course, Drew couldn't help but wonder if he would have made his father proud.

It wasn't something Drew liked to dwell on. His father had died when Drew was still in diapers and learning how to walk. Memories of his father didn't exist, and the things he knew about his father were from what others have said from the past until now.

"I get it," Blake said, pinching the bridge of his nose. "I know how much the rodeo means to you, and I know that I could've done a lot of things differently when Curt left, but I didn't. And I'm sorry."

Drew did a double-take, making sure he'd heard his brother correctly. It wasn't very often Blake apologized, or admitted he was wrong. Mostly because the guy was never wrong, and hardly ever did anything worthy of an apology. All in all, his brothers were good men, and respectable at that. But the way Blake had acted once he took over the ranch, like Drew and Garrett weren't even there and were nothing more than servants of the land…

"If you're wanting to move back onto the ranch, I don't have a problem with that," Blake said, tossing a look at Drew to make sure he was paying attention. He was, no doubt about it. Drew needed the ranch more than he ever needed anything in his life—including the eight-second ride. "But this is your last chance. Don't mess it up."

Drew acknowledged Blake's words with a quick nod.

"I'll have your old cabin move-in ready by three o'clock, once the maid gets here," Blake called out over his shoulder as he made his way back to the main house.

Drew raised a brow, offering his brother a questioning look. "Since when did you hire a maid?"

Blake tossed his head back with a laugh. "Did I say maid?"

Drew shrugged his shoulders and let out a half-laugh, not too sure what was going on.

"I meant Garrett," Blake said with a smirk pulling at the corners of his mouth. He nudged Drew and let out another laugh before saying, "I'm just kidding. If you want your cabin, go get it, but you're on your own for cleaning it. You left it a mess, bro."

Drew nodded with a slight chuckle. He was glad after everything they'd been through, they could still rely on much-needed banter. Garrett had always taken the brunt of their jokes. Not to mention the majority of Blake's pranks, too.

"Once you get settled in, we'll talk about what you can do around here to earn your keep," Blake said, tipping his hat to block the setting sun. "I think I've got the perfect job for you now that I think of it, and it's one that won't require you to use that arm of yours."

Drew wasn't too sure about what job his brother had in mind for him, but as long as he had a roof over his head and food in his stomach, he wouldn't complain.

"Go on and get your stuff unpacked," Blake said, hitching a thumb over his shoulder. "I'm going to finish up a few things and will meet you at the main house in an hour."

Drew opened the door and paused before climbing into the cab of the truck as Blake turned and called out, "And just for the record, I'm glad you're back home."

CHAPTER TWO

Starting over and moving back home was a lot more difficult than the movies portrayed it to be. Thankfully, for Becca Adams, she had a wonderful mother who promised not to let her drown in the mixed emotions of instability and uncertainty.

In a time when everything seemed dark and without hope, her mother provided a light. Becca and her six-year-old daughter, Allie, would live with Carolyn Adams until everything settled down and Becca was back on her own two feet.

The assurance of having her mother's help made the transition from being married with a family, to life as a single mother, as smooth as could be expected. Not that Becca's life was without hiccups. She still had a few kinks to work out. She needed to figure out schooling for Allie, along with finding a job, and how she was going to afford an attorney in order to finalize her divorce from Chad.

The thought of what he'd done crossed her mind every now and then... more often when she had time alone and her thoughts weren't focused on other things—more important things—like getting Allie a bath and tucked into bed, or reading her a bedtime story and scaring away the monsters from under her bed. Allie recently insisted she couldn't live without horse riding lessons, which was just one more thing Becca would need to figure out how to pay for. Of course, Becca's mother assured her that she didn't need to worry about any of that, because she'd already made arrangements with the owner at the Dixon Ranch.

"Good morning, dear." Her mother's greeting pulled her away from her worried thoughts. Becca looked over her shoulder and smiled as her mother walked into the kitchen and took a seat across the table from her.

"Good morning," she whispered quietly, knowing Allie was still sleeping down the hall. It was a little after six in the morning, and Becca wanted an extra hour of alone time before waking Allie and putting a start to their day. "Coffee's made, and believe me when I say it tastes wonderful."

Her mother smiled as she opened a nearby

cupboard and reached for a coffee mug. "The first cup of coffee in the morning is the best, isn't it?"

"Mmhmm," Becca agreed, taking a few more sips before setting her cup down in front of her. She wrapped her hands around the mug for extra warmth and watched her mother stand at the counter and add a couple teaspoons of honey to her coffee.

"Do you remember the youngest Dixon boy?"

Becca raised a brow, wondering where on earth the question had come from, but answered anyway. "Vaguely."

When her mother didn't say anything more, Becca asked, "Why?"

Becca hadn't cared much about the Dixon brothers while she'd been in school. Not so much because she didn't like them, because they'd never given her a reason to dislike them. The difference in their ages had a lot to do with it, though. She scrunched her brow as she tried to remember how much older the youngest Dixon brother was compared to her, but her mother interrupted her math.

"Well, I heard he's back in town now," Carolyn said, turning away from the counter and walking over to the table before sitting down across from Becca. "From what I hear, he had a falling out with Blake soon after Curt moved to Maple Glen to be with Fran. Drew left the ranch shortly after that." She paused for a minute then continued, "Something about the way

Blake ran the ranch and whatever other sibling rivalry was going on between them, but Lord only knows," Carolyn said, waving it off like boys will be boys and there was nothing new. Becca was still trying to figure out what all of that had to do with her, and why her mother had brought it up. Sure, her mother might have thought she cared to be in the know with the latest gossip, but to be honest, Becca couldn't care less.

"The only thing I remember about Drew is how much he loved the rodeo," Becca said, recalling vague memories from her high school days and hearing about the latest rankings and wins at local competitions by Drew Dixon.

Her mother chuckled as she brought her cup to her lips. "Nothing's changed," she said, taking a drink and setting her cup back down on the table. "He still loves it just the same, if not more, than he did back then."

There was no surprise there. Becca knew his type well. Once a cowboy, always a cowboy, which meant late-night rodeos and sweet talking women.

"Allie has a riding lesson coming up soon, doesn't she?"

Becca glanced at the calendar hanging on the wall where she tried to stay up-to-date on the latest events in order to keep track of her ever-changing schedule. Of course, she'd forgotten to write it down.

"No worries," Carolyn said, waving it off. "I'll just give Blake a call after breakfast, and we can go from there."

Becca wasn't quite sure how she felt about Allie continuing lessons, but since her mother insisted that she allow her to continue, she really didn't have a say in the matter. Sure, there had been several valid points Becca had made against Allie attending the riding lessons. One of which had been how dangerous it actually was for a child to be around an oversized, unpredictable animal. It had become a moot point when her mother assured her the men at the ranch wouldn't allow anything to happen to Allie under their watch. They were trained and more than capable of handling the horses while teaching the young girl how to ride and command a horse the right way.

Becca had several more unvoiced opinions in the matter, but her mother reminded her that she'd once been Allie's age, and Becca had once been fond of horses just the same.

"I still remember all the times you'd asked your father to surprise you with a horse," Carolyn said with a smile. "And he'd always tell you that it wouldn't be a surprise if you knew it was coming."

Becca nodded with a chuckle. There had been several times she'd come home from school and had been so disappointed when she didn't find a horse in their backyard. Becca recalled several horse-related memories from her childhood. She'd begged her parents to buy her a horse just so she could be like the girls in her class. Of course, owning a horse had been out of the question because they lived in city limits, and her parents reminded her almost daily that they didn't live on a farm.

The memory of her negotiating with her father seemed to be one of her favorites. She'd tried so hard to get him to buy her a horse, she went as far as telling him that she would scoop poop for the rest of her life. But he still wouldn't budge, and she ended up envying everyone with a horse—including the one and only Drew Dixon.

"I remember your father taking you to the Dixon Ranch once or twice," Carolyn recalled, "and you wanted nothing to do with the horses."

Becca shared a laugh with her mother now. "I remember."

Her mother laughed softly and shook her head. She pulled the cup to her lips and took a drink of coffee before saying, "The look on his face the first time he'd taken you, though... It was priceless."

Becca shrugged as she traced a finger along the curve of her cup. "I think I was more infatuated with the *thought* of having a horse than actually having one stare back at me with its huge eyes while flaring its nostrils. For some reason, they seemed smaller in my mind than standing right in front of one."

Becca's mother laughed at the memory, and Becca could only imagine what her reaction would be now if she were face to face with a horse. Thankfully, she hadn't needed to worry much about it since her mother had offered to take Allie to her lessons the last few times while Becca settled in.

"Well, maybe when you take Allie to her next lesson, you can ask the Dixon boys—"

She cut her mother off before she could finish her suggestion. "Absolutely not. I have no desire to be up close and personal with a horse."

Her mother offered one of her mischievous grins as Allie rounded the corner and entered the kitchen behind them.

"Good morning, Sweet Pea," Becca's mother called out, standing from her chair. She made her way over to the fridge and asked, "Would you like pancakes or French toast for breakfast?"

Becca smiled as Allie climbed into the chair next to her at the table. "Pancakes, please?"

"You've got it," Becca's mother said and shot a wink at Allie. "Would you like to help me make them?"

Allie's face lit up, and Becca's heart melted. The moments the two of them were now able to share with Becca's mother would soon turn into memories neither of them would forget.

"Yes!" Allie said, climbing out of her chair and racing to an empty spot beside her grandmother.

Becca watched the interaction between the two of them, feeling thankful and blessed to have them in her life.

"Wait a minute," Becca's mother called out, tapping a finger against her chin. "Did someone forget to wash their hands?"

Allie's eyes widened as she shot a glance at Becca, who quickly motioned toward the sink and said, "Hurry up. You better get them washed."

After grabbing a nearby step stool, Allie scrubbed her hands in the kitchen sink and dried her hands on a dish towel hanging from the oven door. "All done," she announced, scooting the step stool closer to her grandmother and climbing up beside her to get a better look. "What can I do?"

Becca grabbed a refill of coffee and returned to the table. She enjoyed moments like this when her daughter was growing up and learning how to do things only the "big" kids got to do. Of course, helping in the kitchen wasn't anything new for Allie. She'd been helping Becca since she'd been old enough to lick the frosting off the spatula.

Baking cookies and cakes was their favorite pastime, and living with Becca's mother meant they'd be able to enjoy it all together.

It pained Becca to lose the life she'd had before

leaving Chad. The life she'd made over the last eight years with a man she thought loved her unconditionally, and until death did them apart like they'd vowed. How wrong she'd been about that. She'd once thought she had it all, and she couldn't have asked for a better life. She was married to the man of her dreams, and they'd had a perfectly precious daughter together.

Becca wasn't sure when it all changed, but one thing she knew for sure was the loss left a hole the size of Montana in her heart.

The divorce had taken a lot away from her, but the one thing it couldn't take was the love she had for her daughter. She would do whatever it took to give Allie everything she needed while providing her with the best life she could imagine.

"Let's ask Mom if she would like some pancakes," Becca's mother loudly whispered to Allie. Allie turned to face Becca with a wide smile on her face, holding a spatula in her hand. "Would you like some pancakes, Mama?"

Becca pulled her attention back to her daughter and nodded with a smile. "Of course," she said. "How could I refuse pancakes made by my little girl?"

Allie snickered and turned back around, focusing on the pancake batter as her grandmother poured it into the pan. Over her shoulder, Allie announced,

"You're going to love the shape of your pancakes, Mama."

"I'm sure I will, honey," Becca said, finishing the last of her coffee before standing up and walking over to the sink. "While you're making breakfast, I'm going to hop in the shower. That way, we can start our day as soon as we're done with breakfast."

Becca walked out of the kitchen with the sound of her daughter cheering behind her. She would give anything to keep her daughter happy—even if that meant taking her to her riding lessons and coming face to face with her fear of horses.

CHAPTER THREE

Drew spent a good half an hour evicting dust bunnies and cleaning up the place before heading to the main house. It felt good to be back home, and luckily for him Blake seemed to have welcomed him home without a grudge.

He inhaled a deep breath, taking in the crisp mountain air, and released it slowly as he stepped onto the front porch. He hadn't seen his mother since the day he'd left, and he hadn't given her time to talk him into staying.

His mother was the hub of the ranch, and without her, Drew was certain everything would fall apart. No matter how tough it got over the last few years on the ranch, his mother pulled them through it and reminded them of what life is really all about.

There were several times she stood as referee during brotherly fights, breaking them up and forcing them to make amends before walking away.

He smiled as he pushed through the front door. "Honey, I'm home," he called out as he stepped into the warm, familiar place where he'd grown up. It was good to see that nothing had changed in the year since he'd been gone.

He walked through the living room toward the kitchen where he heard muffled conversation filter through the door. He braced himself for what awaited him on the other side, praying they would be happy to see him and it wouldn't end in a lecture about rodeos and his injured arm.

The smell of baked apple pie greeted him before his mother's smile as he walked into the kitchen. His mother, nearing sixty but who didn't look a day older than fifty, rounded the center island and studied his injured arm before wrapping her arms around him. "I'm so happy you're home," she said with a relieved sigh. "It's good to see you again."

"Same to you, Ma," he said, patting her on the back.

Mama Dixon had been through a lot in the last thirty-some years. From losing her husband to raising three boys on her own, it was a miracle how well she'd held the family together. But the Dixon family was strong, and because of their uncle Curt, they hadn't lost the ranch after losing their father.

Drew hadn't been more than two years old, but Garrett and Blake had been roughly four and six. They had been a little older and wiser than Drew, though not by much, but given the circumstances of their father's death, they had a better understanding.

Drew couldn't explain how it felt being the last to realize he didn't have a father. When Blake and Garrett reached their teens, they'd adjusted accordingly while Drew still struggled to figure things out. He guessed that was just the part of being too young to remember the man they'd called their father.

"Blake was just telling me that you're going to be working the horses and giving riding lessons," Mama Dixon said, glancing between the three of them while she fixed Drew a plate of food. She slid it across the counter in front of him as she said, "I'm not sure you should be out there working anything with an injured arm. You should be lying down and resting. Healing takes time."

Drew caught Blake's slight grin from the corner of his eye and shook his head. "There isn't much I can't do, Ma," Drew explained. "I'm fine with doing whatever is needing done around here."

He wasn't sure what Blake had in mind for him to do around the ranch, but if working the horses was it, Drew didn't have a problem with that.

"You're just lucky to be alive," his mother said as she leaned against the counter. "You have nothing to prove when it comes to those darn rodeos anyway. All they're good for is—"

"Ma," Drew interrupted politely, "I know that you don't like 'em, but I'm fine."

His mother furrowed her brow and pointed at his slung arm. "That's far from fine," she scolded, "and you know it."

Drew swallowed a bite of food and washed it down with a glass of milk, allowing his mother to simmer down a minute. "Doc says I'll be good to go within six months—"

"Or longer."

Drew shot a glance at Garrett, who had stayed quiet through the whole conversation until now. No one needed his two cents, but he was willing to give it to them anyway. Garrett shrugged and went back to clearing his plate.

"And let me guess, you'll be right back to it once the doctor clears you?" his mother questioned, furrowing her brow and waiting for an answer. He couldn't give her the answer she was looking for. An honest answer wouldn't be what she wanted to hear, so instead, he stayed quiet.

She shook her head and tsked, something like their grandmother had done when she was highly disappointed in the choices the boys had made.

"What do you say we finish eating and get out to the stables?" Blake asked, easing the tension that filled the room. "I've got a lot of work ahead of me before I can call it a day."

Drew nodded and finished off his plate of food before going back for seconds. He knew that his mother wasn't happy with the choices he'd made, but he couldn't give up on the rodeo. Competitions were a part of him. They'd been a part of his life for more than half of it, and there was no way he would stop now. Rodeos had become a home away from home.

Drew scraped the remaining food onto a scrap plate for the Wranglin' Duo—a set of Australian Shepherds that ran the ranch right along with the Dixon brothers.

He placed his plate in the sink and waited for Blake to finish scraping his plate before thanking their mother and heading out of the kitchen. Blake grabbed his hat from the hook by the door and put it on, and Drew adjusted his as they stepped out onto the front porch.

Drew wasn't sure about working with the horses with an injured arm even though he knew he could do it one handed with his eyes closed. Horses had always been his favorite, and looking back, he would have tried barrel racing if he hadn't invested so much time and energy in bull riding.

"What do you say we get started for the day?"

Blake asked, patting Drew on the back. The door opened behind them as Garrett stepped outside. He walked around them, mumbling something under his breath before heading down the steps and climbing onto the four wheeler.

Drew hooked a thumb over his shoulder in Garrett's direction and asked, "What's his deal?"

Blake shrugged and said, "I'm not too sure, but it might have something to do with his recent breakup."

Drew glanced over his shoulder and watched as Garrett rode off toward the pasture. Garrett was the fixer-upper around the ranch. He'd fix anything that needed fixed, and they'd called on him a lot throughout the years. More times than not, it turned out the fence needed mending or the gears in their tractor needed tuning.

"I'm glad I don't have to deal with any of that," Drew said, thanking the good Lord for keeping distractions and temptations at bay throughout the years. The last thing he needed was a woman to pull his attention away from the thing he loved the most. "Relationships are nothing but drama, am I right?"

Drew nudged Blake with his elbow, trying to get a reaction out of him. But instead, Blake adjusted his hat and shrugged him off. "I don't know about all that," he said, making his way down the steps. He glanced back at Drew and asked, "Are you coming or what?"

Drew refocused with a nod as he followed his brother down the steps. He thought about his brother's reaction and wondered if Blake had ever started something with that girl from last winter. She'd called and let them know their cattle were in her yard, staring in at her through the dining room window. Blake had gone over there to wrangle 'em up, but it had taken longer than expected. Drew and Garrett had just assumed it was due to Blake and all his sweet-talking ways.

"Do you think you're ready to teach your first riding lesson?" Blake asked as they walked toward the stables.

"Yeah," Drew said confidently. "I was born ready."

Blake slapped him on the back and let out a laugh. Drew felt pretty confident in his abilities to work the horses, and there was no doubt in his mind that teaching riding lessons would be a breeze. At least now the time he'd spent with the horses through the years would count for something.

"That's good because she'll be here any minute," Blake said, tapping the face of his watch. "I think you'll like her."

CHAPTER FOUR

"Are you sure you want to take her?" Carolyn asked, following Becca and Allie to the door. Becca grabbed the car keys out of her purse before slinging the strap over her shoulder. She turned and assured her mother that everything would be okay. She didn't plan on getting up close and personal with the horses.

"What if Allie wants you to walk alongside her while she rides?" Carolyn questioned in a whisper. Becca hadn't had time to think about the *what ifs*. She'd been too busy getting ready at the last minute in order to take Allie to the lesson.

Becca smiled down at her daughter, who now looked up at her with questioning eyes. Of course, she'd heard her grandmother ask a silly question, and now they were both wanting an answer.

"I'm sure Allie will be just fine without me by her side," Becca assured, patting her daughter on the back and shooting her mother a warning look to stop with the questions. "She'll have the trainer by her. I'll be watching from the other side of the gate."

Becca realized how silly she sounded, but she'd seen a horse kick its owner without hesitation, and to be honest, that's all it had taken for her to no longer want anything to do with horses. The only reason Allie was able to go to the riding lessons was because Becca's mother had already paid the owner of the ranch, *and* she promised Allie was in good hands.

Before her mother could ask any more questions, or talk Becca out of going along with Allie, Becca said, "We should really get going, or Miss Allie won't be there on time."

Becca's mother nodded with a smile as she stopped at the doorway. She offered each of them a quick hug and a kiss on the cheek before shooing them along.

"Have a good time, Al," Carolyn called after them. "I'll be waiting to hear all about it."

Allie's face lit up with a smile as she waved back to her grandmother. "I wish you could come, too, Nana."

Becca stopped at the driver's side of the car and looked back at her mother with a smile.

"I'm okay with staying home," Carolyn said.

"You two better get going. I'll have supper done by the time you get back."

Allie climbed into the backseat and buckled in. She didn't say too much on the way to the ranch, but Becca could tell something was on her mind.

"What's wrong, Al?"

Allie looked out the window and offered nothing more than a slight shrug. Becca's heart broke at the sight of her daughter's disappointment. There was definitely *something* bothering her.

"Honey," Becca said, steering the car out of the driveway and down the street. "You know that you can talk to me about anything you want to, right?"

She caught a slight nod in the rearview mirror, followed by a soft sniffle. Allie looked down at her folded hands in her lap, and Becca's heart broke.

She pulled the car over to the side of the road and shifted into park before turning around to face Allie. "Hey," she said, reaching between the seats and grabbing a hold of her daughter's hand. "What's wrong, Allie Bear? Talk to me, hon."

Allie's eyes filled with tears, and if Becca hadn't felt her heart break a second ago, she surely felt it now. "I miss my daddy."

The words were full of emotion as tears streamed down her little girl's cheeks. Becca wasn't sure what to say in response to her daughter's confession, but she knew deep down that her father had chosen another life to live. A life that didn't include them.

Tears stung Becca's eyes, and she forced her emotions under control. Her daughter was too young to understand what had caused her parents to break up and go their separate ways. She only knew how it felt not to have both of them together. Becca knew exactly what her little girl was going through. She'd been in her little girl's shoes when she'd been around the same age. A divorce wasn't easy for anyone involved, but it was especially difficult for kids.

"I'm sorry, baby," Becca said, wishing she had more she could say to make her daughter feel better. She hated that the man she'd fallen head over heels in love with—and settled down and started a family with—had chosen to put an end to everything they'd had and toss it to the side as though none of it mattered. Like Becca and Allie didn't matter.

She didn't care about how the divorce made her feel. She cared more about how Allie felt, and how she was going to get her daughter through the loss of her father when the poor girl wasn't old enough to understand.

"Maybe we can get ice cream after your riding lesson?" Becca said, patting her daughter's hand and offering a sympathetic smile. Tears welled in her eyes, threatening to escape as she waited for her daughter's response. Thankfully, Allie perked right up and wiped the tears from her cheeks as she smiled back at Becca. "I'd like that."

"Me too, baby," Becca said as she turned back around in her seat. "Me too."

She took a deep breath and released it slowly. She checked her reflection in the mirror and made sure the silent tears hadn't streaked her makeup before continuing on their way to the Dixon Ranch.

Becca and Allie were greeted the minute they pulled into the ranch and parked the car. A man she assumed to be Blake met them outside on their way up to the ranch-style house.

Her mother had told her just to knock on the front door and tell them they were ready for their riding lesson. She had assured Becca that they would more than likely be ready. Sure enough, her mother had been right about that as Becca stared up at the cowboy in front of them.

"You must be Becca?" he asked, to which Becca nodded.

"This is my mommy," Allie said, looking proudly at her mother with a wide smile on her face. "And I'm Allie."

Allie laughed as the man tickled her and said, "I know who you are, silly."

The man stepped back from Allie and focused on Becca. He extended his hand in front of him and said, "I'm Blake Dixon, the owner of this ranch."

Becca had assumed right. "It's nice to meet you."

"I've been working with Allie for the last few lessons," Blake said, motioning for them to follow him as he walked toward the pasture. "But my brother, Drew, is back home due to an injury, so I'm going to have him take over Allie's lessons from here. I figured I better make him earn his keep around here."

Blake stopped short of the gated pasture and looked at Becca and Allie. "Are you okay with having my brother take over for me?"

Allie nodded enthusiastically with a bright smile in her eyes. "Yes!"

Blake grinned with a nod. "Alright then, I'll introduce the two of you to Drew and let him take it from there."

Becca's mother had said that Drew Dixon was back in town, but she hadn't believed it until she saw it with her own eyes. He stood off to one side of the gate, propping it open with the toe of his boot while he motioned for her and Allie to enter the horse corral.

"You must be Allie?" Drew asked, tipping his hat against the afternoon sun. The first thing Becca noticed about him was his eyes—as they focused on her. Drew gave her a once-over before righting himself. He cleared his throat and extended his hand. "You must be—"

"Becca Adams," she said, placing her hand in his with hesitance. He sure had changed since the last time she'd seen him. Of course, it had been years ago, but still.

"It's nice to meet you," Drew said, shaking her hand with a gentle squeeze.

His eyes focused on hers, and she felt the heat in his stare. Her cheeks flushed, and she looked down at Allie in order to take cover. She chastised herself for allowing her thoughts to betray her. He was handsome, but definitely off limits.

Blake tipped his hat and said, "Alright, I'm going to head back to the house and finish up a few things. Let me know if I can do anything for you?"

Becca thanked him and turned back to Drew.

"What do you say we get started?" Drew asked, his question pulling Becca out of her thoughts as she watched Allie's face light up with excitement as she jumped up and down. Drew looked from Allie to Becca and asked, "Is your mother joining us today?"

Becca's heart raced and her palms grew sweaty. The thought of being near a horse made her stomach tie in knots. She remembered the last time she had been around a horse, soon after witnessing a man get kicked...

"No," Allie said sadly, "she doesn't like horses."

Drew righted himself, tipping his hat and looking over at Becca.

"It's not that I don't like them," she stammered. She tried to explain the best she could. "It's just..."

She took a deep breath and released it slowly. It was a failed attempt at slowing her heart rate. Drew's eyes focused on her, waiting for her to explain the reason she didn't like horses.

"I used to love them," she explained, avoiding Drew's questioning stare as she focused on her daughter. It was easier to explain as if she were telling her daughter instead of an overwhelmingly handsome man who was now waiting for the reason she didn't like horses. A reason she knew would sound pathetic and without merit. "I'd draw pictures of them for hours, and I'd beg my parents every day to buy me a horse. I'd—"

Drew's laughter from beside them interrupted her. She stood up and spun around, furrowing a brow at him. She wasn't quite sure what he'd thought was so funny. She didn't think she'd said anything that warranted a laugh.

"I'm sorry," Drew said, raising his hands in defense. "It's just that drawing a picture of a horse and owning one are two *very* different things."

Allie chuckled innocently beside Becca. She wanted to tell him that she'd been only eight or nine when she'd had dreams of owning a horse someday, but she bit her tongue. There was no sense in engaging with him over something so silly. It just added one more thing on her list of reasons *not* to like Drew Dixon.

He must have felt the annoyance radiating from her as she stood off to the side and waited for him to get started with the lesson. Once the lesson was over, she'd take Allie for ice cream. But if it didn't start soon, it'd be too late without taking a chance at spoiling supper.

Drew cleared his throat and said, "Alright, then. What do you say we get started?"

Allie clapped and cheered before looking up at Becca. "Will you watch me?"

Becca nodded with a smile. "Of course, baby," she said. "I'll be standing right here the whole time."

She swallowed her fear of something going wrong in the lesson. She tried not to think about the strength of a horse and its unpredictable nature. She knew it didn't matter how tame a horse seemed; it could startle and wreak havoc within seconds. She prayed her daughter would be safe. She also prayed that Drew knew what he was doing.

CHAPTER FIVE

Drew assisted Allie into the saddle after tightening her helmet securely in place. He looked over at Becca, who stood at the entrance on the other side of the gate and watched intently. He had seen the fear in her eyes when Allie had mentioned the horses, and he felt bad for laughing while she explained her reasoning.

If he were to be honest, he felt like a heel for not giving her the chance. He hadn't meant any harm by it. Clearly, his sense of humor was no match for her.

He held a loose grip on the reins as he led Allie and Simon around the corral. "I'm sure you know what to say to make a horse stop, right?"

Allie's eyes lit up, her blonde curls bouncing on her shoulders with each step the horse made beside him. "Whoa!"

Simon stopped instantaneously, and Drew smiled as he offered the horse a good pat on the chest. He'd been close to Simon long before leaving the ranch. Drew had spent hours training the horse, settling him down from his wild days and making sure he'd be one of the best horses they had on the ranch.

"Good job," Drew said, high-fiving Allie while sneaking a glance at Becca, who remained by the gate, unmoved from the spot she was in. Even from a distance, he could see the fear coursing through her. It was as though she was waiting for something bad to happen at any moment. "And what do you do to get Simon moving again?"

Allie smiled down at him, her blue eyes shining in the sunlight. "Yah!"

He chuckled when Simon didn't budge. He didn't even move a muscle.

"Why won't he move?" Allie asked, disappointed in her failed attempt at getting Simon to move. "Yah!" she shouted again, and Drew couldn't hold back the laughter any longer. "That only works in the movies," he said, feeling horrible for laughing. He pointed to her legs and asked, "Did Blake teach you what to do with your legs while riding?"

A puzzled expression filled the little girl's face, and Drew waited for her to come up with an answer. How to get a horse to move forward, slow down, and stop completely were the basics of the riding lessons.

There was no doubt in his mind that Blake had taught the girl those things—the three most important things to know when it came to riding horses—but sometimes it took kids several repetitions to remember them all.

"Squeeze them?" Allie asked, hesitant in her answer.

"Yes, that's right," he said with a smile. He pointed to the area she would need to focus on if she ever wanted to get Simon to move. Drew knew that the strength of her legs wasn't the same as an adult's, but thankfully, it took only a gentle squeeze of the legs to get Simon to budge. "Try it now," he encouraged, and he cheered when she did just that and Simon lurched forward. "See? You did it."

Allie cheered and clapped atop the horse as she called out to her mother several feet away, "I did it, Mama! I made Simon move!"

Becca cheered for her daughter with a nervous smile on her face. "Good job, baby!"

Allie sat proudly in the saddle for the rest of the lesson. Drew kept the lesson simple and all about the basics. From the basic commands to the subtle movements that would remind Simon that he had a rider.

"Do you think my mom will ever like horses again?"

The question came out of nowhere, blindsiding him and leaving him without a response. He wanted to answer Allie's question, but he didn't know the reason her mother didn't like horses in the first place. He mentally kicked himself for interrupting Becca by making it a joke. He should have let her keep talking. He would have a better idea on how to get the girl's mother to let her guard down and relax a little bit more while watching her daughter's lessons.

"I'm not sure," he said, catching another quick look at Becca as they neared the entrance. "Do you think she will?"

Allie sighed and shook her head. "I don't think so, but I want her to ride with me."

Drew walked over to the gate, allowing Allie to say the command needed to stop Simon. Becca took a few giant steps back, and Drew saw the fear in her eyes as they got closer. "Whoa, buddy," Drew said, grabbing the reins and gently guiding the horse away from Becca.

"Are you done with your lesson, baby?" Becca asked, and Drew heard the shakiness in her voice.

"Yep," Allie said confidently, reaching out for Drew as he helped her off the horse's back and steadied her on the ground. He watched as Allie raced up to her mother and wrapped her arms around her waist. He smiled at the interaction, all while trying to figure out how to approach Becca about her fear of horses. "Drew told me they only say 'yah' in the movies, but it doesn't really work," Allie explained, looking back at Drew with a wide smile on her face.

"That's right," he confirmed as he sent Simon off and approached the gate. "Don't worry, we'll stand over here," he said to Becca, pointing to the other side of the gate as he closed it behind him.

Becca offered him a soft smile and asked Allie, "Are you ready for some ice cream?"

Allie's eyes lit up at the reminder of Becca's promise. "Can Drew come for ice cream, too?"

Drew's heart stopped the minute she asked the question, and for whatever reason, he immediately looked at Becca and wished he hadn't. The look on her face told him what her answer was before she could even say it. She looked as though Allie had invited a monster to join them for ice cream instead of the kind-hearted gentleman that he was.

Instead of being offended, he made it easier for Becca and said, "I'm sorry, kiddo, but I'm gonna have to pass on that invite for today. I've got a lot of work to get done yet."

Allie's disappointment lingered far longer than he'd liked it to, but he knew he was making the right choice. Becca didn't like horses, and it was obvious she didn't like him all too well either.

"Maybe next time you come for your lesson, I'll have ice cream here with you," Drew said, hoping that would lift Allie's spirits so she wouldn't be so disappointed. At least he knew by the girl's invitation that she liked him. That made him feel a little better, too. "How does that sound?"

Allie nodded and looked up at Becca. "Can I get a triple scoop of double chocolate chip?"

And just like that, the girl had forgotten Drew had turned down the invite to get ice cream with them. He watched Becca release the breath she must have been holding as she agreed to her daughter's request.

She turned to Drew and offered a soft smile, one that barely reached her eyes, and said, "Thank you."

He wasn't quite sure what she was thanking him for, but he nodded with a tip of his hat anyway and watched as the two of them made their way back to the car.

There was something about Becca that caught his attention, other than the fact she didn't like horses, which was an understatement. The look on her face as he brought Allie and Simon over to the gate to meet up with her had told him that Becca was deathly afraid of horses. There was no doubt something had happened to make her scared like that, and for some unknown reason, he wanted to be the one to ease her fears. He just didn't know how to do that without getting close to her. The last thing he needed was to get too involved and not be able to walk away.

CHAPTER SIX

Becca took a deep breath and released it slowly as she climbed into the driver's seat and started the car. There was something about Drew that had caused something to stir inside of her, and she couldn't blame it on the panic she'd felt when the horse had galloped right up to the gate where she'd been standing.

No, it was something entirely disconnected from the incident with the horse. It had everything to do with the way he'd not only handled the riding lessons with Allie, but Allie's invitation for ice cream.

"Are we leaving?" Allie asked from the backseat.

"Yes, baby, we're leaving," Becca said, glancing over her shoulder and making sure her little girl was buckled in before shifting the car into drive. She steered the car along the gravel, following the circular driveway back to the highway. Once they were headed into town, Becca made light conversation with Allie—an attempt to get her mind off of Drew. She would not allow herself a minute longer to think about him.

"What do you say we just grab our ice cream and take it back to Nana's?" Becca asked, knowing there was a slight chance Allie would refuse her offer and want to go inside the shop while enjoying their treat.

"But we can't eat ice cream in front of her," Allie said with a furrowed brow. "That wouldn't be nice."

Becca's heart melted with how thoughtful her daughter truly was. "Of course not. We'll bring her some, too."

Allie seemed to like that even better and relaxed in her seat. Becca smiled and said, "I think she'll like that, don't you?"

Allie nodded her head enthusiastically and said, "Mmhmm."

"Good deal," Becca said. "We can all enjoy ice cream while you tell Nana all about your riding lesson. I'm sure she's excited to hear all about it."

Allie's eyes lit up and she said, "I can tell her all about it."

Becca nodded as she pulled her car into the line at the drive-through window. She would order their ice cream and head home for the night. She had things to do later on that she had been putting off, but for now, she would enjoy ice cream with her mother and Allie.

"Nana," Allie called out, racing through the front door with two ice cream cones in her hands. "We brought you something."

Becca followed Allie into the house, stepping inside off the front porch and shutting the door behind her. Allie's excitement ricocheted throughout the house as she searched for her grandmother.

Becca pulled up a chair at the kitchen counter and settled in while waiting for Allie to return with Becca's mother. It didn't take long for the two of them to enter the kitchen, both donning wide smiles on their face. "You didn't have to bring me anything," Becca's mother said, "but thank you. It tastes wonderful."

Allie climbed onto a chair next to Becca and licked at the melting ice cream. "I can't eat mine fast enough," she said, trying with all her might to slurp up the ice cream before it could make a mess on her hands and the counter.

"Would you like a bowl?" Becca's mother asked, already making her way over with a bowl and sliding it across the counter in front of Allie. "Sometimes it's hard to eat it fast enough, and the summer heat doesn't help matters."

Allie nodded as she plopped her cone upside down inside the bowl her grandmother had given her. She didn't hesitate another minute as she reached for a spoon and dug in.

"So… tell me how riding lessons went today," Carolyn said, looking from Allie to Becca with a smile. Becca knew her mother enjoyed taking Allie to the riding lessons, and she wondered if it would have been better to allow her mother to continue taking Allie. The idea of her mother taking Allie instead seemed better now that she'd not only met Drew, but also nearly had a panic attack right in front of him. The fear she had of horses was something she couldn't control, and she hadn't planned to express that fear in front of anyone, especially not her daughter's trainer.

Becca listened as Allie told her grandmother all about the commands she'd learned, and how she rode Simon around the corral and was able to control the horse with just a slight movement of her legs. As Becca listened, she realized her little girl was no longer the little girl she'd once been.

"And Mom got scared when me and Simon came to the gate," Allie explained, leaving Becca wishing her daughter hadn't brought it up.

"Simon and I," Becca corrected with a smile, wondering if that would be enough of a distraction to change the subject. But it wasn't. Instead, her daughter accepted her correction with a carefree laugh and continued, "I like Drew. We're going to have ice cream the next time I see him. He couldn't come with us today. He had a lot of work to do at the ranch."

Becca focused on her ice cream, knowing her mother was looking at her for some kind of confirmation of what Allie had told her. Nothing her daughter mentioned was wrong, but Becca knew her mother was curious to know more.

"Yep, that about sums it up," Becca said, ignoring her mother's questioning look as she continued eating her ice cream. Just before Becca could change the subject, her daughter interjected with unexpected news.

"And Drew and *I* think that Mom should take riding lessons with me," Allie said, proudly emphasizing her correct grammar, along with the idea that she and Drew had come up with together.

Becca finished her ice cream in one last bite as she slightly shook her head, giving herself a minute to process what her daughter had just announced. Her heart sped up at the mention, and she wasn't quite sure what scared her more—the horse or being close to Drew.

Allie finished her ice cream and hopped down from the counter. "Can I go play outside with Rosie?"

"Yes, but wash your hands and face first, please?" Becca called after her daughter as she watched her leave the kitchen. She was thankful her little girl was making friends with the neighborhood kids, and Rosie was definitely a sweetheart and just a year older than Allie.

"I don't think that's too bad of an idea," Carolyn said, finishing the last of her ice cream as she grabbed a washcloth from the kitchen sink. She ran it under the water and brought it over to the counter. No matter how hard Allie had tried not to make a mess, drops of ice cream still managed to find their way onto the countertop. Becca eyed her mother, wondering what on earth she was thinking. As though her mother could feel the intensity of Becca's glare, she looked up and met Becca's eyes with her own. "Really, I don't see anything wrong with getting you out there with Allie and overcoming your fear of horses."

Becca swallowed past the lump that formed in her throat. She was a grown woman who had overcome a lot in the last few months, let alone becoming a single mother in a blink of an eye. Overcoming her fear of horses was not something on Becca's list of priorities at the moment.

"I don't think I want to," Becca admitted. "I'm perfectly fine watching Allie's lessons from the gate and keeping my distance."

Her mother shot her a knowing look and nodded. "I think I know what *this* is all about," Carolyn stated matter-of-factly. Becca crossed her arms over her chest, refusing to give in and accept riding lessons. "But that's neither here nor there," Carolyn said, tossing the washcloth into the sink and making her way back over to the counter. She pulled up a chair across from Becca and said, "The only thing that matters is whether or not you're present for that little girl."

Becca was taken aback by her mother's statement. By the assumption that Becca could possibly be flaking out on her daughter just because she refused to overcome her fear of horses. "I'm here, aren't I?"

She choked back the emotion, knowing her mother hadn't meant to strike the nerve she had. Her mother was her best friend, her sounding board, and the one who gave Becca advice when she was at her wit's end.

"You are," Carolyn said, "and I didn't mean to make it sound like I think you're not. I just know how hard it is to be present when your mind is everywhere but here in the moment... where it matters the most."

Tears stung Becca's eyes as she fought to hold back. She'd been through the trenches and back, and had managed to keep it together thus far. She wouldn't allow herself the chance to break now. Not when she wanted to believe that everything would get better—*was* getting better.

"Honey, I know what you're going through isn't

easy," Carolyn said, reaching out and placing a warm hand on top of Becca's. "I've been there myself. I know how hard everything has been, and I know that the uphill climb isn't over for you yet."

Becca squeezed her eyes shut, willing the tears away and praying the dam wouldn't break.

"But you need to find something to take your mind off the bad things for a while," Carolyn stated, and Becca knew deep down her mother was right. Becca had been so focused on getting out of her marriage with Chad, she'd been caught up in a rush of mixed emotions that were hard to handle alone. She'd spent too much time thinking about her marriage—where things had gone off track, what she had done so wrong to cause the love of her life to cheat on her, and, not to mention, how she was going to get through it all on her own.

"I think spending time at the Dixon Ranch will do you and Allie both some good," Carolyn stated, offering Becca a quick pat before climbing off the chair and hurrying to the oven. "Oh shoot, I forgot all about the lasagna."

The smell of burnt food filled the room, and no sooner had her mother opened the oven door than a cloud of smoke exited the oven. Smoke alarms sounded throughout the house, each detector squawking loudly.

Becca rushed to the light switch, flipping it on and

pulling the chain for the ceiling fan in the dining room. With any luck, the fan would pull the smoke from the kitchen and within a short amount of time, it would clear.

While her mother busied herself with the burnt food, Becca searched for the source of the incessantly loud screeching. As she reached for a smoke detector, Allie raced into the house with Rosie, both covering their ears and shouting over the screeching. "What's happening?" Allie asked before pulling Rosie back out the front door.

Becca silenced the smoke detector and rubbed her ears. Between the constant squawking of the alarms and the girls' shouts, her ears hurt.

"Nothing to see here but burnt supper," Carolyn said, showing off the pan of lasagna with burnt cheese and overflowing sauce. "Perhaps we should order out tonight?"

Becca offered a slight smile. "Perhaps we should."

Her mother placed the burnt lasagna on top of the stove and cracked the kitchen window. "You round up the girls, and I'll clean this up so we can go," Carolyn offered. "It'll be my treat."

Becca nodded before making her way to the front door. The girls were playing with Barbies on the front porch when she opened the screen door and asked if they'd like to go out for supper. It took only a second for the girls to run off the porch in the direction of Rosie's house to ask if she could have supper with them.

Becca waited on the front porch, thinking about what her mother had said. She hated to think that her mother was right about overcoming her fear of horses, and what good it would do her to get her mind off of the divorce. Maybe her mother was right and it wouldn't hurt Becca to talk to Drew the next time she took Allie to her riding lessons.

CHAPTER SEVEN

Drew looped his arms through the plastic bags and carried the groceries he'd gone to the store for into the main house. Had his mother not mentioned being short-handed on a few ingredients for her homemade apple pie, Drew would have forgotten about his promise to Allie about ice cream.

"What's all this?" Blake asked, rummaging through the bags once Drew set them down on the kitchen counter. Without missing a beat, Blake answered his own question. "Ma must've sent you on a run to the store."

Drew shuffled around the small ranch-style kitchen, attempting to get the gallon of ice cream in the freezer before it melted. It was surprising that it hadn't melted on the drive home. Summers in Montana were no joke, and without running AC in his old Chevy pickup, it was a wonder he hadn't melted either.

Once he'd saved the ice cream, he stood in front of the fan and aired himself out. The drive into town and back hadn't taken longer than twenty minutes, but it was just long enough to work up a sweat.

"Did you get enough ice cream?" Blake hollered out while digging through the freezer for ice to fill a cup. Drew tossed his brother a glance over his shoulder. "Stay out of it," he said, stepping away from the fan and making his way back into the kitchen. "It's for Allie when she comes back for her riding lesson."

Blake put the carton of ice cream back and closed the door with a smile on his face. Drew knew exactly what his brother was thinking, but he hated to be the one to break it to him—he wasn't getting attached. He was just being nice.

"So, let's talk about Becca for a minute," Blake said as he filled his glass at the kitchen sink and motioned for Drew to sit down. Drew wasn't sure he wanted to talk about Becca. He wasn't quite sure how he felt about her, but he wasn't about to find out either.

"What's ice cream with Allie got to do with Becca?" he asked, pulling out a chair at the table and sitting down while waiting for his brother to take a seat across from him. "The girl invited me to go along with them for ice cream, and judging by the look on Becca's face, I had no choice but to decline the little girl's offer."

Blake raised a brow at him, but he defended himself yet again. "Hey, I'm not lying when I tell you that Simon isn't the only one Becca doesn't like."

"Is that so?"

Drew wasn't going to go into all of the details, because at the end of the day, it didn't matter. Becca hadn't liked him from the get-go, even as far back as he could remember from their high school days as well. She'd been a few grades below him, but he still remembered her. After he graduated, though, he hadn't given her much thought.

"Anyway," Blake said, leaning forward in his chair. Drew was thankful for the change in subject. Maybe his brother would let him off the hook about Becca, and they could talk about things that actually mattered, like the auction coming up and the new horses that needed to be welcomed to the ranch. "I'm thinking about offering her a job here."

Drew snapped his attention away from the calendar on the wall and focused on Blake. "Offer her a job?"

He could have kicked himself the second the

question left his mouth. It wasn't his decision to make about whom to hire around there.

"Given her situation—"

"Situation?" It was obvious Drew didn't know everything that Blake did, but he still couldn't wrap his head around it. "What kind of situation could she possibly be in that she'd need to take a job here?"

"It's none of my business, to be honest," Blake said, sitting up straight and tossing back the last of his ice water. Drew focused on Blake, waiting for him to explain.

"But it's enough of your business to offer her a job?"

Blake cleared his throat and stood from the table. Drew waited as Blake refilled his cup and leaned on the counter. "Well, you remember Carolyn Adams," Blake explained, crossing his arms in front of him, and Drew nodded. Of course he remembered Carolyn. She had been his eighth grade teacher. "She mentioned it would do Becca some good to get out of the house and clear her mind of some things."

Drew wasn't sure what those things were, but like Blake had said, it wasn't any of their business. Besides, if Becca wanted anyone to know, she'd tell them.

"Alright," Drew said, trying to figure out just what Blake had in mind for her to do. They didn't really need much help, aside from the cattle and horses. Garrett had a good hand on the maintenance of the place when he wasn't busy running with the fire department. And Drew knew for a fact the woman wouldn't want anything to do with tending the horses—no matter how many times Drew told her there was nothing to be afraid of. When Blake didn't say anything more, Drew asked, "What are you thinking she could do around here?"

Blake shrugged and finished off another glass of water before dumping the ice into the sink. They had a long day ahead of them, and the heat was just getting started. Drew stood from the table and followed his brother out the screen door and onto the front porch where two wooden rocking chairs sat waiting for them.

They both sat down at the same time, overlooking the pasture to the north of the main house. Drew caught sight of Garrett, running alongside the fence line with the four-wheeler and knew he must be checking for breaks. The cattle were a force to be reckoned with when it came to that fence, and from the looks of it, it had required more repairs than Drew could count on both hands.

"I think Ma could always use some help with meals and cleaning," Blake said, and Drew agreed with a slight nod. "She spends a lot of time cooking for us, and I hate to think of the time she spends picking up after us."

Drew heard that. He gave his mother props for raising the three of them without their father, and as much as he hated to admit it, they needed to learn a thing or two about picking up after themselves. Unfortunately, he'd never been too tidy. But on the other hand, washing dishes or folding laundry wasn't below him. He'd be willing to help his mother any day of the week.

"But honestly, I don't think Becca would mind the job offer," Blake said, tossing a questioning look at Drew. "Do you?"

Drew wasn't sure what to say in response to his question. He barely knew Becca, let alone whether or not she would be willing to take the job. "Cleaning up the lodges and cooking meals?" Drew asked with a shrug. "I don't see why she wouldn't."

But in all fairness, the thought of her turning it down had crossed his mind the moment Blake mentioned it. Drew wasn't too sure about a lot of things in life, but he knew it was hard to find a woman who wanted to work on the ranch. They came few and far between, and Drew had yet to find one.

"I guess all we can do is talk to her about it the next time she's here with Allie?"

It was more of a statement than a question, so Drew nodded along with Blake as they both turned their attention to Garrett. He was riding back toward them, holding down on the throttle of the ATV with a frustrated look on his face.

"This can't be good," Drew said, standing up and heading for the steps. He wasn't sure what was going on with Garrett, but he'd be the first to find out.

CHAPTER EIGHT

Thumbing through the small-town newspaper, Becca searched for something to catch her eye in the help wanted section. There were plenty of odd-and-end jobs, mostly for teenagers, but nothing stood out for a twenty-eight-year-old, recently divorced, single mother.

She sighed and flipped to the last page. Her mother had told her that she didn't need to worry about finding a job. She'd been told to take her time and settle in before stressing herself out. But of course, all of that was easier said than done, especially since Becca hated the fact she'd had to move back home in the first place.

Fighting back the tears, Becca took a deep breath and closed her eyes. She'd never once thought she'd end up moving back home. Not in a million years had she ever thought her dream life would come crashing down and turn into a nightmare.

She'd been told time and again not to let the blame fall on her shoulders, but how could she not? The weight of the divorce was heavy and it was enough to crush her.

"Mama," Allie called out as she raced into the kitchen and made a pit stop right next to Becca. Becca quickly swept away the shed tears and offered a half-smile at her daughter. "Yeah, baby," she said, tucking a strand of her daughter's curls behind her ear. Allie made being a mother easy. She was the child Becca had spent nights praying for while struggling through the battles of infertility and treatments. The challenges her marriage had faced, along with her own battles of defeat, had taken their toll over time. But the battle scars seemed to disappear when they'd found out they were expecting a baby girl. Prayers had been answered, and Becca couldn't thank God enough.

"Are you crying?" Allie asked, turning her head sideways in an attempt to see Becca's face. Becca closed her eyes and laughed, trying her best to keep it together in front of her daughter. The last thing she wanted to do was put worry into her precious girl's thoughts.

"Mama's fine, baby," she explained. "I'm just tired, is all. I didn't sleep too well last night."

Allie wrapped her arms around Becca and squeezed tightly. Becca lifted the girl onto her lap and kissed the side of her face. "Have I told you lately how much I love you?"

Her little girl brought a pointed finger to her lips and offered a mischievous grin. "I don't think so."

"I think so." Becca laughed as she brought out the tickle monster and tickled her daughter's sides until she was in a fit of laughter. She would never tire of the sound of Allie's laughter. It was music to her ears, and almost like a release for her worries.

"Can I go play at Rosie's?" Allie asked after recovering from Becca's attack. Becca smiled and said, "Just as long as you're on your best behavior while you're over there."

Allie's smile met her eyes as she climbed off of Becca's lap. "I'm always my best, Mama."

Becca winked and tucked another loose strand of hair behind Allie's ear before kissing her forehead. "Okay, then go on and have fun. Be sure to check in after a while, please," she called after her daughter as Allie raced out of the kitchen.

Becca stared at the folded newspaper lying on the table in front of her. She knew there wasn't a single job listed for her to take, but she couldn't help looking through it one more time.

"Please tell me you're not doing what I think you're doing."

Her mother walked into the kitchen, catching Becca fumbling with the paper in front of her. "Looking for a dog?"

"You can't fool me," Carolyn chastised, making her way over to the table to join Becca. She watched her mother sit down and waited for the lecture. Not so much a lecture, because her mother had never been one to harp, but it still felt a bit like that. "Talk to me, Bec."

Becca released a slow breath and combed a hand through her hair. She had so much to focus on, but finding a job was at the top of her list. When she didn't say anything, her mother said, "You know that I've got you covered for however long you need it."

Tears stung the back of Becca's eyes as she pushed back her emotion. She wouldn't break down, not now. Not when she was trying to be strong.

"I know how hard it is starting over," Carolyn assured her, reaching out and grabbing a hold of Becca's hand. "I also know how refreshing it is to have someone to lean on and help you through it."

Becca nodded, swiping the fallen tears from her cheeks. She grabbed a napkin from the center of the table and dabbed her eyes, hoping Allie wouldn't come marching in the front door anytime soon. The last thing she needed was for her daughter to see her like this.

"I know," Becca said, releasing a slow breath and willing herself to pull it together.

Her mother offered a gentle squeeze of her hand and smiled. "You're going to be just fine. I've got a good feeling about what's ahead for you and Allie," she said, wrapping both of her warm hands around Becca's hand. Becca dabbed at a few more tears with her free hand and nodded. She wasn't quite sure what the future held for them, but she knew her mother wouldn't let her fail—never had and never will.

"I had a talk with Blake the other day, actually," Carolyn said, releasing Becca's hands and scooting back from the table before standing up. Becca watched as her mother grabbed two cups from a nearby shelf and filled them with sweet iced tea. "I know I've told you plenty of times not to worry about working, but I also know how hard it is for you to sit on your hands."

Carolyn slid the cup of tea in front of Becca and said, "And I know that you're afraid you'll never have enough." Becca tried to interrupt her, but her mother held up a finger and continued, "It's not a bad thing to realize how much you lost during your divorce."

Becca relaxed at her mother's words. She felt defensive when it came to her life then and now. There was no doubt that her mother knew what she was going through—she'd been there herself. Becca's only fear was that she wouldn't find anything comparable to what she left behind.

"Look, sweet pea," her mother said, resting a hand on top of Becca's. "What you lost isn't as important as what you've gained."

Becca thought a moment about her mother's words. She couldn't shed any more tears than she had the last few days. Maybe her mother was right. Maybe it was time to stop looking at the bad and focus on the good. There were several things Becca should be thankful for—and she had them right there with her, all under the same roof.

She swept a loose strand of hair away from her face as she took a drink of tea. It was time to put one foot in front of the other and continue making her way through the tragedy that had once been a dream.

"From the sound of it, Blake might have something for you to do at the ranch if you're willing to do it," Carolyn said with a soft smile. "I know you're not too fond of the ranch life, but it's something to take your mind off of things."

Becca's thoughts went straight to Drew Dixon, but she shook them away when she realized what her mother was telling her—she wanted a job, and she could have it.

CHAPTER NINE

Drew didn't mind helping Garrett mend the fence, but this time, the cattle had done a number on it. It would take more than a couple of hours to repair what the two-thousand-pound animals had done.

"Think it's time to switch to something a little more reliable?" he asked Garrett, who was a few feet down the line and working hard at mending the wire.

Garrett mumbled something about how it didn't matter when it came to the cattle, but Drew lost focus when he caught sight of Becca's car pulling into the drive off the main road.

He wasn't sure what she was doing there, but he did know that Allie sure didn't have a riding lesson lined up for the day.

"I'll be right back," Drew said, pulling off his

work gloves and shoving them into his back pocket. He slapped his brother on the back and heard him mumble something yet again, but Drew wasn't having it. His attention was on the attractive brunette stepping out of the car and making her way to the main house.

The sundress she was wearing today was a softer yellow than the one she'd worn the last time he'd seen her, and this one flowed loosely around her curves and hung just right on her sun-kissed skin.

Drew picked up his pace, trying to make his way to the front porch before she had a chance to knock. If anyone was going to help her, he wanted to be the one.

Allie climbed out of the backseat, catching sight of him right away before running toward him. He tipped his hat, angling it just right to block the sun from his eyes. Allie came to an abrupt stop in front of him, her curls coming to a halt right along with her.

"Hey, Drew," she said, looking up at him with bright blue eyes. "I was wondering if I can ride Simon today?"

Drew looked toward the main house where he'd last seen Becca. She was making her way toward them when Allie said, "I know it's not my day, but Mom is here to talk to Blake, and I just want to ride Simon."

Becca approached them and offered Drew a shy

smile as she placed her hands on the little girl's shoulders. "I'm sorry," she said, keeping her eyes on his. "I told her not to bother you when we pulled in."

He watched Becca's eyes scan the damaged fence behind him. He turned and gave it a quick look, seeing that Garrett was still busy working on it. He turned back to face her and said, "She didn't bother me. I was actually coming to say hi when I saw you guys pull in."

The wind caught a strand of Becca's hair, and he fought against reaching out and brushing it away. Instead, he looked down at Allie and said, "I guess it wouldn't hurt to get Simon out for a while. You can ride as long as your mother doesn't mind."

He looked from Allie to Becca and waited for Becca to agree or disagree. "I mean, if you're going to be busy talking to Blake, it won't hurt for her to be out here," Drew said, not wanting to ask what she had to talk to his brother about. "And you know what else we can do while the grown-ups talk?"

Excitement lit up Allie's eyes as she looked from her mother back to Drew. "What?"

He inhaled a deep breath and let it out in a rush as he said, "I bought ice cream just for you."

He heard Becca's breath hitch, and he took a minute to figure out if maybe he'd done something wrong. Maybe Becca didn't want Allie to have sweets all too often. Maybe he made the mistake of assuming it would be acceptable.

"But," Drew added, "you have to ask your mother if it's alright before we can have some."

He felt proud of his correction, pulling it from the tip of his tongue as quickly as he had, and from the look on Becca's face, she appreciated his respect. He knew that mothers had the final say, and he wasn't about to go against Becca's parenting.

"That's fine," Becca said, fidgeting with the hem of her dress as she swayed from side to side. She pulled her eyes away from his and focused on Allie. He followed suit and looked down at Allie as Becca said, "Just don't eat too much. I don't want you to get an upset stomach while riding Simon, okay?"

Allie nodded enthusiastically as she jumped up and down. Drew smiled when the little girl looked up at him with a wide smile on her face. "Mom says I can."

Drew took a quick look at Becca who offered another shy smile. Drew couldn't help but chuckle as he nodded and said, "Alright then, let's get to it."

Excitement radiated off the child as Drew led them toward the main house. He was close enough to Becca for the breeze to waft her scent right by him. It was a mixture of honeysuckle and something else he couldn't quite put his finger on. Not that it mattered.

It was a good scent, and he would enjoy smelling it every time she came around.

"I'll get the ice cream scoop right after I find Blake for your mother, okay?" Drew asked Allie before making his way from the kitchen to the living room in search of his brother. Allie stood tall by the refrigerator, acting much older than she actually was, while Drew disappeared from the kitchen. He would enjoy having ice cream with Allie before taking her on a ride around the pasture. He hadn't much time to think about what he would teach her on such short notice, but had decided that maybe they would ride together in the saddle and he'd take her for a tour of the ranch.

Once he found Blake, Drew walked back into the kitchen and dished out two scoops of ice cream for Allie and offered some to Becca, but she politely turned it down.

"Okay, more for us, then," Drew teased, shooting a wink toward Becca before asking Allie, "right, Allie?"

"Uh huh," Allie said, sliding in next to him and helping herself to some ice cream.

Drew helped her grab it before taking his own and walking toward the front door. He shot a glance at Becca, who was now talking to Blake about possibly working around the ranch. Drew was more than happy to hear her tell Blake she would take the job. But at the same time, it would get a lot harder for him to keep his distance from her.

CHAPTER TEN

Becca relaxed as she leaned against the gate to the pasture and watched Drew and Allie ride the horse. She hadn't been too sure that Drew would allow Allie to ride when they first arrived since she didn't have a lesson that day, but Becca had been thankful he'd agreed to let her.

Her mother had offered to keep Allie at home with her, but Becca felt bad for always relying on her. Carolyn had a life to live and didn't always need to stay busy with Allie. Plus, it didn't hurt to bring Allie along. For the most part, Allie minded well and Becca hardly ever had to scold her.

Becca's only worry had been whether or not Allie would hear her conversation with Blake about taking the job. She wanted to have a conversation with her daughter later on about the job offer and what that would mean for their time together. She knew Allie would understand. It wasn't like Becca hadn't worked outside the home before now. She just wanted to make sure Allie knew what to expect.

Allie would be starting school once summer was over anyway, and the time she'd spend there, Becca would be busy cleaning and making meals at the ranch. It would all work out.

"Hey," Drew called out from atop the horse behind Allie. Allie was wearing the brightest smile Becca hadn't seen in a while. "How'd your talk with Blake go?"

Becca looked up at him, keeping her distance from the horse, and shielded her eyes from the sun with her hand. "It went well," she said, unsure how much Drew actually knew about his brother's offer. "How'd the ice cream taste?"

She hadn't asked anyone in particular, but both of them responded. "Great."

"You should've had some, Mama," Allie said, leaning forward in the saddle as Drew climbed off the back.

Becca watched with bated breath as she waited for the horse to do something unthinkable. Thankfully, the horse stood its ground and calmly waited for the two riders to climb off its back. Becca released the worried breath.

"I will next time, baby."

Becca waited patiently by the gate as Drew guided Simon away from where she was standing. She was more than thankful he remembered how she felt about horses, even though she couldn't imagine how anyone could forget when she'd reacted the way she had.

"Drew took me down by the creek and around the pasture," Allie stated confidently. "He said that we could just enjoy a nice, easy ride instead of working."

Becca caught Drew staring at her as he made his way back over to them. His eyes were dark brown, and his smile aligned well with the dimple in his cheek. She felt warmth radiate into her cheeks as she pulled her eyes away from him and focused on her daughter. She silently chastised herself for allowing herself the freedom to notice how handsome Drew Dixon was. He could be handsome all day long, but he was still the reckless, carefree cowboy she knew wouldn't stick around for too long.

"Did you tell your mother about the cattle?" Drew asked Allie, making his way over to the gate and pulling it open to allow Allie to sneak past him as she rushed out and wrapped her arms tightly around Becca's waist. "Mama, the cattle are huge," Allie said, drawing out the word in reference to how big she thought they were. Her daughter hadn't been around too many farm animals. It had been a few years since they'd visited a petting zoo, and even then, cattle hadn't been the animal of choice.

"And Drew says they keep breaking the fence," Allie stated matter-of-factly, standing proudly in front of Becca. Becca could tell her daughter was more than okay with the ride she and Drew had gone on while she stayed back at the house and talked to Blake. Her daughter enjoyed learning new things, and apparently, Drew was a jack of all trades when it came to teaching Allie a thing or two. "He says they're going to work on getting the fence repaired tonight, but he thinks they need a stronger fence."

"Is that right?" Becca glanced up from Allie and met Drew with her eyes. He offered a sly grin and a soft shrug of his good shoulder. "From the way it looks, I'd say he might be right."

Becca had seen Garrett working hard on the fence when they had first pulled into the drive. At least before Drew had pulled her attention away.

"It won't be long before they're in our freez—"

"Shh," Becca cut him off, holding a finger to her lips and praying he didn't say another word. She knew life on the ranch was the way of life in Montana, and she also knew the cattle were not only a source of income, but also a source for food as well. But that didn't mean she wanted her six-year-old to hear all about it. She was still innocent and didn't need to think about the fate of the cattle once their purpose on the ranch was met. "How high was the creek?" she asked innocently, an attempt to change the subject before Allie caught onto what Drew had said.

Drew swiped his cowboy hat off and ran a hand through his dark brown hair. She wasn't sure he'd liked it too well when she made him stop mid-sentence, but she would explain later when they weren't in earshot of little ears.

"Well, judging by the fact we haven't had much rain all summer, it's fairly low," Drew explained, leading them toward her car. Becca hated the thought that went through her mind just then as she followed closely behind Drew. She didn't want to leave just yet. She wanted to stick around and enjoy the moment. She'd be working around the ranch day to day, and if she was going to be cleaning up after the Dixon brothers, she might as well get used to them. "It's pretty much nonexistent."

Becca nodded, knowing her question might have come across as ridiculous. She knew the creek she'd loved as a kid ran dry through the summer and flowed high in the early months of the year after the spring rain.

"Did she tell you about the flowers she picked for you?" Drew asked, looking from Becca to Allie for confirmation. Allie hadn't mentioned anything about flowers to Becca. And from the looks of it, if she had picked flowers, they were no longer with them.

"I picked pretty blue and purple flowers for you, but Simon made me drop them," Allie explained, jutting out her bottom lip.

"He did, did he?" Becca questioned, quirking a brow in Drew's direction. She wasn't sure she wanted to know what Simon had done to cause her daughter to drop the flowers she had picked, but there was something telling her that she needed to know. If Simon tried to buck them off his back, Becca would call it quits on horse riding lessons right then and there.

"Yep, he did," Allie said, and Becca looked to Drew for further elaboration since her daughter wasn't being too forthcoming with the details she desperately wanted to hear.

They watched Allie run off toward the tire swing. Drew tipped his hat and leaned against the porch railing. "It's not at all what you're thinking, Bec."

She felt her heart skip at the way he said her name, but Becca quickly dismissed it. "Simon's a good horse, but he doesn't know the difference between wildflowers to eat and wildflowers for mamas," Drew explained, offering a slight chuckle as Becca realized she'd gotten herself worked up before knowing all the details. "I wouldn't put Allie on a horse if I thought for one minute it wasn't safe. Trust me."

Becca studied him for a minute, willing herself not to tell him that trust didn't come easily for her. That she couldn't fully trust him to do the right thing when the last man she'd given her whole heart, and eight years of her life to, had done the opposite.

Thankfully, interruption came in the form of a slamming screen door behind them as an older woman stepped onto the front porch carrying a pie. Becca knew just from the conversation she had with Blake that the woman standing in front of her, offering her a homemade apple pie, was none other than Mama Dixon.

"Blake told me that you'll be helping out around here?"

Becca nodded with a smile, thankful that her daughter was off playing on the tire swing hanging from a nearby tree. "That's right," she confirmed.

"Well, the good Lord knows I'm not getting any younger, and this ranch ain't slowing down anytime soon," Mama Dixon explained. Becca knew the woman had to be in her late fifties, close to her sixties. "It'll be good to have you here with us."

"Go ahead and take this pie as an offering of gratitude for accepting Blake's offer," Mama Dixon said, extending the pie in front of her. Becca offered the kind woman a soft smile and accepted the apple pie.

"And just know that I'm looking forward to having you here."

The excitement in Mama Dixon's voice awoke an excitement in Becca's heart. She couldn't wait to work alongside the woman, helping out wherever she was needed. As far as she could tell, her mother had been right about busying herself and getting her mind off things.

"I guess I should add that the pie might also be a peace offering ahead of time for having to deal with Drew," Mama Dixon teased, giving Drew a slight nudge. Becca glanced between them, waiting for him to correct his mother, but instead, he grinned and shook his head. "He's hard headed, but he means well."

"Ma, come on," Drew said, and Becca tried her best to hide her laugh. "She doesn't care about all that."

"Not yet anyway." Mama Dixon winked at Becca but dismissed the fact she'd even mentioned it with a wave of her hand as she turned and headed back to the porch steps. Becca didn't have the heart to tell the woman she was wrong. There was no way Becca was getting involved with anything Drew Dixon. "I better get back inside. Don't want the pies to burn," she said, hooking a thumb over her shoulder toward the door. "It was nice meeting you, Becca."

"Same to you, Mrs. Dixon."

Mama Dixon waved a hand and said, "None of that. You can call me Mama Dixon just like the rest of them around here."

Becca nodded and watched as the woman went back inside.

Drew turned back to Becca and chuckled. "Alright, then," he said, looking down at his boots as he kicked at the gravel. "I better let you two get going before Ma sends you home with more pies."

Becca nodded with a laugh. She loved the fact that Mama Dixon offered her a fresh baked pie, and the fact she couldn't wait for her to start at the ranch. It was a good sign—a hopeful sign—that everything might be okay.

Allie raced over to them from the tree she'd been playing on and asked, "Are we leaving yet?"

Becca wanted to remind Allie of her manners but was interrupted by Drew. "Be sure to add a dollop of ice cream after you warm that pie up," he said, pointing at the pie in Becca's hand. "It makes Ma's pies all that much better."

Allie's eyes lit up once she realized what Drew was saying. She studied the pie in Becca's hand and asked, "What kind of pie is it? Can we have some when we get home?"

"It's apple, baby," she said, switching the pie to the opposite hand and bringing her daughter close with the other. "We'll have some tonight after dinner.

How about we tell Drew thanks for everything today?"

Allie smiled with an affirmative nod before turning toward Drew. "Thanks for everything today," she said proudly, matching her mother word for word. Becca offered Drew a shy smile, hoping he knew just how thankful they were for the riding lessons. "And thanks for the pie, too."

Drew adjusted his hat, keeping his eyes on Allie he said, "I'm not the one to thank for the pie. The Lord knows I don't bake."

Allie stared back at him with a confused look on her face, and it didn't take Drew long to explain that his mother was the one to thank for the pie because she had been the one to do all the baking. With that, Allie looked up at Becca and asked, "Can I go inside for a minute, Mama?"

Becca nodded, knowing what her daughter was going to do. She smiled as she watched Allie race up the steps and into the house. It wasn't long before she heard Allie call out for Mama Dixon, and the two of them returned to the front porch.

Mama Dixon held the screen door with her hip as she dried her hands using the apron she was wearing. She looked down at Becca and said, "She sure is something cute. Coming in here just to thank me for the pie and ice cream."

"Now wait a minute," Drew said, tapping his

finger on the railing. "I'm the one to thank for the ice cream."

Allie let out a burst of excitement through laughter and shook her head. "Thank you everyone for everything. There," she said, turning toward Becca, "can we go home now, Mama?"

Becca laughed at her daughter's ability to put on a show and was more than thankful for the manners. "Of course," Becca said, offering one last thank you to Mama Dixon for the pie, and a thank you to Drew for watching over Allie while she was busy talking about the job with Blake. "Have a good night," Drew called out from the front porch as Becca slid into her car.

"You too," she called out before shutting the door. She waved a hand over her steering wheel and smiled before checking to make sure Allie was buckled in and ready to head for home.

She hadn't felt too confident about a lot of things since moving back home to Woodford Creek, but right now, while sitting in the driveway of the Dixon Ranch, she felt hopeful. A newfound hope that whatever was coming her way was going to be something worth more than the price she'd had to pay in the past. She couldn't afford to lose much more, but hearing her mother's words in her thoughts, Becca knew she had everything to gain.

CHAPTER ELEVEN

Drew backed the trailer up to the gate and shifted the truck into park. He hopped out of the driver's seat and made his way to the rear of the trailer. Happy with the distance he'd left between the gate and the trailer's door, he reached into the cab of his truck and killed the engine.

He'd spent the last two days preparing the ranch for what was coming, knowing he was the only one excited to break a new horse. His brothers had their doubts, voicing their thoughts over breakfast, but Drew promised it would all work out. Soon, they would have another good working horse, and one more to offer up for riding lessons.

He wouldn't mention the thought he'd had of adding another horse with Becca in mind. That would be pushing his luck. Aside from that, he'd tried real hard to keep her out of his thoughts.

Drew made his way to the back of the trailer. He could hear the frustrated breathing of the horse inside. The incessant whinnying followed by short bursts of hot air told him it was time to get the horse out of its cage.

The horse slammed its body against the inside of the trailer, stomping madly and rocking it side to side.

"Easy, boy," Drew said, keeping his tone light and his posture at the ready. He'd thought about bringing over a couple of the ranch hands when he arrived but dismissed the idea. He'd taken on bulls weighing more than the horse locked inside the trailer. He would manage.

Opening the gate to the corral, he propped it open before turning back to the trailer. He stepped toward the door, reaching out and thinking about his plan of action once the horse was free.

He'd watched the horse for a good ten minutes before loading it into the trailer and heading back home. Right from the start, he knew what he'd gotten himself into. But as he'd told his brothers—he was up for the challenge. Besides, he was getting bored just hanging around with a bum arm. He needed something to keep him busy, and the new horse fit the bill.

He steadied himself and blew out a slow breath to calm his racing heart. No sooner had the horse reared up inside the trailer, causing a ruckus before the real fun even began, than his adrenaline kicked in.

"Alright, here's the plan," Drew said out loud, preparing not only himself, but the horse as well, for what was about to happen. "This can go one of two ways, dude. You can either leave the trailer nice and calm without a fight, or I'll have—"

"Do you always talk to the horses?"

Becca's voice was soft but filled with concern as she watched from a short distance. She offered him a shy smile, and he looked around for Allie. "She's with my mom. They're spending the day baking cookies and watching reruns of the *Frozen* movie."

Drew had no idea what movie that was, but all that mattered was Allie was having fun. "Well, hopefully she remembers that I like cookies."

A smile pulled at her lips, and he would swear she was the most beautiful woman he'd ever seen. "I'll be sure to remind her about that," Becca said, keeping the smile on her face as she walked toward him.

The horse stomped and reared inside the trailer, startling Becca and causing her to jump back.

"Maybe you should get someone to help you?" Becca suggested, her eyes wide with concern. Drew shifted his weight and said, "He's nothing I can't handle. I've rode bulls bigger than him. He's just ready to get out of the trailer he's been cooped up in for the last few hours."

Becca slowly nodded, but she didn't look too convinced Drew could handle his own. He didn't have anything to prove, though, and he knew he wasn't one hundred percent capable of handling the horse if it decided to do something crazy—at least not with a slung arm.

Tipping his hat, he went along with what Becca had suggested. It would be a fool's move to unload the horse by himself, and honestly, he knew that. But he also knew everyone was busy doing their own thing around the ranch. And besides that, they weren't too thrilled with his decision to bring the horse to the ranch in the first place, let alone wanting to help him with it.

"Alright," he said, lifting his hat and running a hand through his sweat-filled hair. He'd been standing out in the midday sun for a good hour now trying to come up with a game plan in order to unload the horse. It was time to call over some help to keep him from looking like a fool in front of Becca. "I'll round up some help."

Becca's shoulders relaxed, and she tipped her head back almost as though she was relieved he wasn't as stubborn as he was letting on. Almost as though she was thanking God that he'd given in and was smarter than he looked.

"I was starting to think you're a glutton for punishment," Becca called out as he grabbed his phone out of his pocket.

He hit the button on his phone and brought it up to his ear as he poked a finger into his chest and asked, "Who me?"

Becca shook her head with a laugh.

The deep voice on the other end of the line told him he'd called the right number. "Hey, Mason, I'm gonna need some help down here," he said. "Do you have a minute to lend a hand?"

At Mason's acceptance, Drew ended the call and shoved the phone into his front pocket. He could always count on Mason.

It took him less than five minutes to get to the corral, and in those few minutes, Becca had told Drew she was heading inside to visit with Mama Dixon and see if she needed any help today.

"I still think you're a fool for bringing this one home," Mason said, shaking his head as he readied himself on the other side of the trailer.

"Well, I did, and he's here, so now help me unload him," Drew said with a sharp tone. He was ready to get the horse out of the trailer and into the open area of the corral. It wasn't doing any good keeping the horse locked up inside.

Mason saluted him before readying himself at the door. The minute Drew shifted the latch to open the door, Mason reached for the rope and steadied the horse with Drew's help. The horse reared, showing them who's boss, but not for long if Drew had anything to say about it.

Mason released the rope once the horse was inside the corral and the gate was closed, leaving them on the outside looking in. He shot Drew a look, and Drew knew what he was thinking before he even said it. "You've got your hands full with this one."

Drew watched the horse round the corral, galloping wildly and with reckless abandon. He studied the horse for a good while as he kept his distance. Mason could believe what he wanted, but Drew had a good feeling the horse would break and end up being one of the best.

"You good?" Mason asked, pulling Drew's attention away from the horse. Drew nodded, feeling fairly confident he could hold his own from here on out. The horse would have space; Drew would make sure of it. Over time, and little by little, the horse would warm up to him—or at least that's what he hoped.

"Alright then, I'm heading back to the cattle," Mason said, offering a quick wave before hopping onto the four wheeler and taking off.

Drew leaned into the fence and rested his arms on the top of the railing. He studied the horse for a while, waiting for it to burn off some of its steam and pent-up energy.

He glanced over his shoulder, in the direction of the main house, wondering if his mother had put

Becca to work already. He knew having her there would do them some good, especially for his mother. The last thing he wanted was for his mother to work so hard in providing the meals and doing all of the cleaning. They'd been talking about hiring a maid for the lodges, but that idea had been dropped numerous times through the years. It just wasn't in the budget to hire more than they could handle well enough on their own. But, like his mother had said, she wasn't getting any younger, and the ranch wasn't slowing down anytime soon.

He let his thoughts trail off and focused back on the task at hand. He needed to take his time with this one, and he didn't need anything, or *anyone*, distracting him.

The black horse seemed to have settled quite a bit over the past hour, and Drew wondered if it was time to make a move.

He readied himself near the gate, taking in the horse's movements and watching its mannerisms. The guy who had owned the horse had told him there had never been any problems with bucking or biting, but Drew knew that was then and this was now. The horse didn't know him from Adam, and aside from just the change in scenery, everything was different now.

Drew pulled at the latch on the gate and slowly opened it. He took his time entering the corral, keeping his eyes on the horse as he stepped inside.

The horse didn't seem to mind Drew being there, which was a good sign. At least he wasn't anxious to charge at Drew and take him out. The last thing he needed was another injury to set him further back… and further from getting back to the rodeo circuit.

"Easy, boy," Drew said in a soft tone whenever the horse would trot by him. "Let's give you a name while we're waiting."

He'd thought about a few names to give the horse on the drive back home, but there weren't too many that fit him. The horse was reckless and carefree, and aside from that, Drew could also tell the horse had a soft side. He'd give the horse a name that suited him, without having to worry if it didn't fit his personality.

Each time the horse trotted by, Drew carefully extended his good arm, reaching out for the horse and taking it slow. The sooner the horse realized Drew didn't mean any harm, the sooner they could get started with the training.

Drew thought about Allie just then. If she were there, he would have asked her what she thought the horse's name should be. There was no doubt in his mind, as he studied the horse, that the little girl would have been thrilled to help name the horse.

Drew hesitated for a minute, wondering if perhaps naming the horse could wait another day, until Allie could see him at least. He was all about making the young girl's day, and if he thought ice cream had done it, he knew naming the horse would top that.

His thoughts went back to Becca, though. There was no way she would allow Allie to be near a horse as rough as this one, but maybe he could talk her into letting Allie hang out by the corral and name him from afar.

The horse stopped in front of him, dark, wide eyes stared at Drew. The horse seemed to be sizing him up, but Drew didn't budge. If he moved an inch, the horse would take it as a threat, and who knows what would happen after that.

Instead, Drew used his words, along with the tone of his voice, to soothe the horse. He'd spent years working with Simon, shaping him into the horse he was today. He could do the same with this one as well. No doubt, it would take a lot more time, but in the end, it would be worth it. The ranch would have another well-trained and reliable working horse in no time at all—give or take a few months.

"Easy, boy," he said again, keeping his tone light and his eyes focused on the horse. His heart raced inside his chest, barreling against his ribs as he waited for the horse to make the first move. It could easily go one of two ways, and Drew could only hope whatever way it went, it was in his favor.

CHAPTER TWELVE

"Mind if I help?" Becca asked, making her way over to the kitchen sink where Mama Dixon busied herself with the morning's dishes.

Mama Dixon slid over, making room for Becca to join her. "I'll never say no to help."

Becca rinsed while Mama Dixon washed in silence for the first few minutes, at least until Drew caught their attention from the kitchen window in front of them.

"He's had a way with horses," Mama Dixon said, handing Becca a plate and carrying on, "ever since he was a little boy… about four or five, he thought he had what it takes to change a horse."

Becca watched Drew for a minute, listening to

Mama Dixon while rinsing the plates before placing them next to her in a drying rack.

"I swear he'd be the one to tame a wild horse if he could," Mama Dixon said with a proud smile. "There aren't too many who have a love for horses like my son, Drew."

Becca stayed quiet, nodding along with the woman, continuing to rinse while she washed and talked highly of her son's talent with horses. Becca had seen firsthand the love Mama Dixon recalled about Drew. The bond she'd witnessed between Drew and Simon had been enough to calm her worries about Allie's riding lessons.

"He might seem a little rough around the edges," Mama Dixon said, handing her one cup after another as she talked. "But he's got a heart bigger than Montana when it comes to the things he cares about."

Becca nodded along, listening to Mama Dixon carry on about Drew and how proud she was, not only of Drew, but all of her boys. They had turned out to be quite the gentleman, if she could say so herself. Becca knew a mother's love was deep, and more than that, it was unconditional. She could not only see it, but she heard it in Mama Dixon's voice as well.

Becca caught a few glances every now and then while helping with the last of the dishes. She watched with concern as he stood against the railing and held his hand out in front of him.

Mama Dixon must have seen it too, because she stopped mid-sentence and rested her working hands over the sink.

Neither of them said a word as they watched Drew. Becca prayed the horse wouldn't do anything foolish. It didn't matter that at one time she couldn't stand the thought of Drew… she'd had a change of heart. And besides, she didn't want to see another man get injured by a horse. Once had been enough, and she still didn't trust horses because of what she had seen all those years ago.

She watched with bated breath as the horse approached Drew. It was obvious the horse was skittish, and that made the thought of what could happen next even worse.

The horse eased its way closer, timid and docile, until it nudged Drew's hand with its nose. They watched as Drew extended his hand, gracing the horse's nose with a single touch before the horse veered off in the opposite direction. Becca slowly released the breath she'd been holding.

"That one's going to take some time," Mama Dixon said, continuing on with the last of the dishes. Becca was silently thanking God that the horse hadn't hurt Drew. She knew the day was still young, and Drew would more than likely be working with that horse until the sun set behind the mountains. But now, after seeing the horse's hesitance followed by the mere curiosity it had, she could breathe a little easier while she finished rinsing the last of the dishes and placed them into the rack.

"Thank you for your help, Becca," Mama Dixon said, drying her hands on the towel hanging in front of them. "How long are you planning to stick around?"

Becca dried her hands on the towel, caught off guard by the woman's question. If she meant for the day, the answer would be easy—for however long Mama Dixon needed her. She'd planned to stick around for most of the afternoon, helping where she could and getting familiar with how things were at the ranch. Her mother and Allie would be busy most of the day, which gave Becca plenty of time.

"However long you need me," Becca replied confidently. She already liked Mama Dixon from the get-go, and just knowing she was there to relieve some of the woman's workload had been enough to keep her there after accepting Blake's job offer.

Mama Dixon let out a hearty laugh as she made her way around the kitchen. Becca watched as she gathered ingredients from a nearby cupboard, a couple of pans from the cabinet on her left, and began throwing together a few things over the stove. "If that's the case, you'd never leave, dear," she stated matter-of-factly. Becca knew the woman wasn't joking about the workload. She could only imagine what it was like from sunup to sundown around there. Becca had only seen a small section of the ranch, and its workers, though she knew there was more to see and learn.

"But for right now," Mama Dixon carried on, interrupting Becca's thoughts of what to expect at the ranch. "I'll have you help me gather a few things around the kitchen as I make lunch. We've got quite a few men out there who are sure to be getting hungry."

Becca smiled and went along with Mama Dixon's instruction, grabbing a few ingredients out of the fridge so she could set them down at the counter next to the stove. Becca snuck a few glances out of the kitchen window on her way by. Drew was still busy with getting the horse to trust him. She thought about it for a minute while standing near the window. How much effort was Drew willing to give just for the horse to trust him?

"You'll see him in a few minutes," Mama Dixon called out, pulling Becca's attention back to where it needed to be. She didn't need to busy her thoughts with how well Drew handled the horses, or how patient the man truly was. She should have known better than to be caught staring out the window like a teenage girl. She righted herself and finished carrying the milk and butter over to the counter and set them down. Heat crept into her cheeks as she waited for Mama Dixon to call her out on her interest in Drew. "I'm surprised the butter hadn't melted."

"I'm sorry," Becca said hesitantly. She felt foolish for allowing herself to be carried away by the thought of Drew Dixon, let alone being caught staring at him by his mother.

"No need to be sorry," Mama Dixon said, "but you'll have time to catch up with him when you take his lunch out to him."

A sly smile crept onto Mama Dixon's face as she continued cooking lunch, and Becca knew what the woman had to have been thinking. She wanted to tell her that she was wrong. She had no interest in Drew. Not like that. She was going through a divorce. Just got out of a bad relationship. She didn't want to pursue anything with Drew Dixon. Not now, not ever.

"So, tell me a little bit about yourself," Mama Dixon said, placing the grilled sandwiches onto the plates lining the counter. "I know you were born and raised here and Woodford Creek, but then you ran off to Billings with what's his name…"

"Chad," Becca said, cringing at the taste his name left in her mouth. She hated saying his name. Hated the thoughts it brought along with it. She was full of hatred, and hurt. She couldn't figure out what she had done so wrong to deserve what happened.

"Yes," Mama Dixon said. There was a pause. A moment of silence reigned as they let the awkwardness of the situation surrounding Becca's return home hang around them. "I'm sure Carolyn is thrilled to have you back home. I'm sure she just adores that little baby of yours."

Becca swallowed the emotion threatening to escape as she nodded along with whatever Mama Dixon was saying. She'd thought about how she would explain her situation, tell people about her divorce and the reason she was back in town. But all of that was apparently a lot more difficult than she'd thought it would be.

"You've done a wonderful job raising that little girl," Mama Dixon said, handing a plate to Becca with a smile. "She's got manners for miles, and she sure is a cutie patootie."

"Thank you," Becca said. "It sure hasn't been easy these last few months..."

She let her words trail off, realizing she wasn't quite ready to open up about any of her hardships to a woman she barely knew. No matter how inviting it was to confide in someone other than her own mother, she didn't want, or *need*, to be the subject of the town's gossip. Even though she had a good feeling that she might have already been.

"Well, anytime you need a break," Mama Dixon said with a soft smile, "you can bring her to me. I'll gladly keep an eye on that little sweet pea anytime."

Becca thanked her as she tried her best to hide the

emotion the woman's words brought with them. "I appreciate that."

Mama Dixon affirmed her offer with a slight nod and shooed Becca out the door with the grilled chicken sandwich and homemade potato salad.

Becca made her way down the porch steps, careful not to drop the plate of food or the can of soda. She inhaled a deep breath as she focused on where she was headed.

She spotted Drew in the middle of the corral, standing in the bright summer sun, with his shirt hanging off his shoulder. If there was one thing she didn't need… it was Drew Dixon looking as good as he was now.

CHAPTER THIRTEEN

Drew caught sight of Becca headed his way and pulled his shirt back on. He wasn't one to stand half-naked in front of a lady. No matter what people liked to believe, he still had common decency.

He struggled into his shirt, pulling it down as he approached the gate.

"Hey, what brings you out here?" he asked, already knowing the answer because of the plate in Becca's hands. She handed him the plate of food and turned to leave.

"Bec," he called out, stopping her before she could make a beeline straight for the house. When she turned to face him, he smiled and asked, "Wanna take a break with me over there under the tree?"

He watched her look off in the distance where a

picnic table was positioned underneath an old maple shade tree. He was shocked when she nodded. "I'll share my lunch," he said with a slight nudge and a wink.

"You don't have to do that," she said, taking a seat across from him at the wooden table. "I'm not all that hungry. I can wait until I get home to eat something."

He refused to eat in front of her as he handed over half of his grilled chicken sandwich. "That's a long time to wait and eat. Besides, Ma makes the best food around here."

He was happy when she accepted the other half of his sandwich. He wasn't one to eat in front of anyone, and aside from that, there was something about Becca Adams that made him want to know her better. He couldn't seem to shake her from his thoughts, and no matter how many times he'd told himself not to, he couldn't help but wonder about her story and what had brought her back to Woodford Creek. Aside from what he had already heard from the rumor mill about her leaving her husband and moving back home with her mother, that is. He wanted to hear it from her firsthand, but he also didn't want to come off as nosey or pushy. At the end of the day, it was none of his business.

Becca had no sooner taken a bite than he'd asked, "How are you liking working with Ma so far?" He apologized, giving her a minute to answer. She dabbed her mouth with a napkin and said, "This is really good."

He smiled proudly at his mother's ability to cook a decent meal. "Told ya that you'd be missing out."

Becca nodded and set her half-eaten sandwich down. "Your mom is so sweet," she said with a smile. "She reminds me of my own mother, actually."

Drew could see that. Carolyn and Beverly were only a few years apart in age, and both were excellent examples of what mothers should be. "I know that she took a liking to little miss Allie already," Drew stated matter-of-factly as he took a bite of food. He washed it down with a drink of soda and said, "She can't stop talking about how enjoyable it is to have her around."

Becca smiled as she chewed the last of her sandwich. Drew wondered if his mother had gotten around to telling Becca how much she adored her little girl. His mother was fond of children, wanting to take them all under her wing and show them everything there was to know about country living. It would be only a matter of time before his mother would do the same with Allie—*if* she hadn't already started.

"She's mentioned how much she adores Allie," Becca said. "She's offered to keep an eye on her, too."

Drew nodded along as he finished off the rest of his lunch. There was no doubt his mother would offer to look after Allie, and it only made sense now that

Becca was working right alongside them at the ranch. He knew his mother would enjoy every minute.

"I'm sure that will help you out. Being a single mother can't be easy," Drew said, and no sooner had he said it than Becca's expression changed from hopeful to something he couldn't quite explain.

She crumpled the used napkin into the ball of her fist and looked down at the table in front of them. "No, it's not, but I'd like to think I'm doing the best I can."

He swallowed hard, taken aback by the torment in her voice. He hadn't meant to make her question her efforts. He hadn't intended to even broach the subject, let alone talk about it.

"I'm sorry, I didn't mean—"

"It's okay," she said. She looked up and met his eyes with hers. And for just a split second, he caught a glimpse of the storm raging in her eyes before she looked away. "It's not your fault. And it surely isn't a secret that my life falling apart is what brought me back to this small town."

Her words were heavy with hurt, and it made Drew want nothing more than to comfort her and tell her that even though that might be true, it didn't define her. She was still capable of living a good life.

Before he had a chance to say anything, she wiped a stray tear from her cheek and leaned back. Instinctively, he reached out and grabbed her hand, causing her to pause a minute.

"Bec, I didn't mean to bring it up," he said, surprised she didn't immediately pull her hand away. "I'm sorry. And as far as I can tell, you're better for it."

She offered a shy smile and whispered, "Thanks."

"I'm not too sure what happened to bring you back home, but I do know that whatever it was, it wasn't good for you and Allie," he said, keeping his hand on hers.

"It wasn't supposed to end like that," she softly whispered, looking past Drew. He held onto her hand for as long as she allowed him to as he patiently waited for what was coming. He wasn't sure what kind of life she'd left behind, but he knew without a doubt she would be okay. She rolled her eyes and let out a heavy sigh as she wiped away the fallen tears. "Look at me, falling apart. You've got better things to do than to listen to my sad story of a man cheating on me and deciding we weren't good enough for him anymore…"

Her words trailed off, and Drew knew she'd said more than what she'd planned on telling him. He couldn't believe any man would want to cheat on a woman like her, and not to mention leaving a little girl in the mix of it.

"I'm sorry," she said, sliding her hand out from

under his before standing up. She wrapped her arms around her front and looked off in the distance.

He stood up, not wanting her to think she'd said too much or said something wrong. "You have nothing to apologize for, Becca."

He meant every word, whether she believed it or not.

He closed the distance between them, offering her a shoulder to lean on if she needed it as emotions raced through her. He hated that he'd brought it up. He hated that the thought of everything she'd left behind brought so much pain.

"I'm sorry," he said, reaching out and pulling her close to him. It was a move he knew he'd later regret. A moment he realized he'd be unable to take back. There would be no turning back from the way he felt about her now. He wanted her to know he would be there for her no matter what.

She hesitantly wrapped her arms around him and allowed him to hold her. It only lasted for a minute, but it had been long enough to spark something inside of him. A connection he hadn't felt with anyone until now.

"Everything's going to be alright," he said. He wasn't quite sure how true his words were given her situation, but he meant them, and right now, that's all that mattered.

She gently pulled away from him, righting herself

and wiping away the tears that had fallen from her soft hazel eyes. "Thanks," she said, taking a step back. "I'm sorry... I shouldn't have—"

"It's okay," Drew said, knowing she was regretting opening up to him. "It happens to the best of us."

She offered a half-smile as she nodded. He watched her release a heavy sigh as she stared off at the mountains in the distance. Drew could only imagine the turmoil in her thoughts. He couldn't imagine what life would be like to lose it all and have to start all over again from the ground up. And, just to think, not even a month ago he'd thought his life was over just because of an injury. Becca's whole life had changed due to an unforeseeable action caused by someone who vowed to love her forever. Not only Becca, but Allie too.

That thought alone made him want to prove he was a better person than that. He would move the Rocky Mountains to make sure Becca and Allie knew they had people to rely on—they had *him*.

"What do you say we take a walk to the stables and visit Simon?" he asked, knowing there was a chance she'd refuse. Instead, she surprised him and went along with him as he tossed the paper plate into a nearby trash can and headed toward the stables.

CHAPTER FOURTEEN

Becca walked alongside Drew, close enough to question the racing of her heart. He'd held her hand and allowed her the chance to tell him everything. Regardless, she still found the control to keep most of it bottled up inside. She didn't want him to know everything. Especially the mess she truly was because of how lost she'd felt when her ex had cheated on her. How heartbroken and alone she'd felt while crying herself to sleep at night.

She'd told herself several times over the last few months to pick herself up off the floor and not allow a man to have that much control over her emotions. But that had been easier said than done.

She'd only just met Drew, aside from the times she'd known him from school, and she wasn't about to give him a reason to think she was crazy. That she didn't have things figured out, because she honestly didn't. She would be lying if she said she knew what was coming next. She didn't have the slightest idea.

They walked toward the barn, and she tried her best to silence her thoughts. He was taking her to the stables. The stables where they kept Simon, and she wasn't quite sure she was ready to meet the horse up close and personal just yet. She wasn't sure if she'd ever be ready.

She thought of what had transpired between the two of them at the picnic table. The way he had held her hand, patiently waiting for her to tell him everything. The look in his eyes as she expressed emotions she'd refused to show anyone. She hated crying. She hated showing how weak she truly was, or how emotional the divorce was making her.

"Are you ready?" Drew asked, pulling her out of her thoughts and back to the moment. They were standing in front of the bright red building. It was now or never. Becca knew deep down she needed to overcome her fear of horses. She needed to let go of everything and move forward.

She nodded, inhaling a deep breath and releasing it slowly as Drew pulled open the wide wooden doors and motioned for her to enter the building.

"It's okay," Drew said, leading her into the barn and past the empty stalls. "I'm not going to let anything happen to you. I promise."

Becca wanted to believe him. She wanted so badly to trust him because he'd been so good with Allie, but she couldn't shake the dread forming at the bottom of her stomach as it twisted into knots.

"Can I just stand here and look at him from a distance?"

She could hear the fear in her voice, and she regretted allowing it to show. Drew wasn't pushing her toward the stall with the large horse, but she could tell how badly he wanted her to trust him.

She took one more step forward, willing her nerves to settle as she stayed close to Drew's side. She jumped when Simon whinnied, and Drew chuckled beside her. "It's not funny."

"I'm sorry," he said, holding her close as they stalled for a minute. "It's just a sound horses make. There's no need to be so nervous."

She knew he was right, but then again, she also knew that horses had the power to hurt someone if they truly wanted to. Her thoughts shifted back to her ex as she thought of all the ways he'd hurt her. He had held the same power over her that she was pinning on the horse.

"It's okay," Drew said, willing her to take one more step toward the stall. He held tightly to her hand, encouraging her to make the move, while letting her know he wouldn't let anything happen to her.

"I'm right beside you," he promised. "Nothing's going to happen. Simon's the best horse I've ever had, and there's no chance he's going to hurt you."

With Drew's promise, Becca inhaled a deep breath and slowly exhaled as she neared the stall. Simon hung his head over the edge, curious to see who Drew had brought with him as he lifted his nose in the air and more than likely caught the scent of her.

Drew guided her toward the stall, slowly introducing her to Simon and lifting her hand to meet the horse's muzzle. There, standing close enough to Drew and reaching out to Simon, Becca felt a rush of emotion as she pushed past her fear and tried her best to relax. She held her breath through the beating of her heart as it raced inside of her chest, and she waited for the horse to make a random move.

Only Simon hadn't moved. Instead, he stood perfectly still as if he knew she was deathly afraid and didn't want to spook her. She wasn't sure what she would do if Simon decided he'd had enough, but she felt comforted with Drew by her side.

She ran her hand up and down the length of Simon's muzzle, relaxing with each stroke the horse trusted her to make. She released a slow breath, realizing she was overcoming one of her biggest fears.

Sure, she wasn't anywhere close enough to the horse to trust it one hundred percent, but standing there now, right where she was, was enough to make her realize she was capable of overcoming anything.

"See?" Drew said, smiling at her as he rested a hand on her lower back. "You're doing it."

She laughed now. Letting the rush of everything escape as she brought her other hand up to stroke the other side of Simon's face. The horse was gentle and as patient, as Drew had promised he would be.

"Simon." She whispered the horse's name and watched as his large eyes stared back at her. They were dark and mysterious, but full of compassion and understanding. The love she had for animals hadn't died the day her fear had been born. The love she had was stronger than ever now as she stared back at the horse in front of her.

"Next, we'll take you for a ride," Drew said with a confident smile. Becca shook her head, refusing the idea of climbing into a saddle. That would be where she drew the line. "What do you think, Simon?"

She took a step back from the stall and shook her head. "I don't think that's a good idea," she said, suddenly filled with the anxiety and fear she'd thought she'd let go of. "Maybe next time, but not today."

She took a step back, willing herself to stay strong and continue refusing Drew's offer. No matter what he said or how much he promised, there was no way she was going to climb into the saddle.

She took another huge step back, creating some distance between her and Simon, when she tripped over something behind her and stumbled backward.

Drew rushed to her side and caught her before she hit the ground. He held her close for a minute and made sure she was okay. She stared into his brown eyes, and for a minute, she witnessed a look she'd never seen from him until now.

"You've got to be more careful," he said, with concern edged deep in his tone. "There's a lot of hidden opportunities around here, and you'll end up kissing hay if you're not careful."

She wasn't quite sure what kissing hay would be like, though she hated to find out. But that didn't stop her from thinking about kissing Drew as he held her close and stared into her eyes.

A million thoughts went through her mind, and she knew the last thing she should do was kiss Drew Dixon. He grew closer now, leaning in to meet her lips with his.

Her heart pounded inside her chest as she willed herself to breathe. He was close enough to kiss her, and she wasn't sure it was a good idea. They weren't ready for that. *She* wasn't ready for that.

Drew Dixon was everything she wasn't. He was carefree and reckless. She was reserved and hesitant. He took risks and chased adrenaline-filled events. She shied away from change and would choose safety over everything else—including the safety of her heart. It had already been broken once, and she couldn't take the chance for it to break again.

"I'm sorry," she said, backing up while making sure she watched her footing. The last thing she wanted was to trip while trying to make a run for it. "I can't…"

She turned and headed for the door, leaving Drew behind her and praying he wouldn't follow her. The last thing she needed was to explain all the reasons they couldn't make it work. She was broken, and she had more than just herself to think about. She had to think about Allie, and how Allie would react to Becca falling in love with someone other than her father. Her little girl didn't know any better and was still processing her parents' separation. The last thing Becca wanted was to cause any more conflicting emotions, and that included her own.

"Becca, wait," Drew called out behind her as she left the stables. She kept walking, willing herself to keep moving forward and resist the urge to turn back around. "Becca, I'm sorry. I shouldn't have…"

His words trailed off as she kept walking. She wanted so badly to turn around and tell him that he had nothing to be sorry for. It was her, not him. It had everything to do with the past she tried so hard to forget, but couldn't, because the man she'd married had been a part of her life for eight years. She couldn't let go of the pain and the hurt he'd caused her, let alone allow herself to fall for another man who might do the same thing. She couldn't tell him those things because she knew there was a chance Drew would tell her that she was wrong about him. And she knew there was a part of her that would believe him... and once she believed him, there was no turning back. She would want everything to work out, and she knew nothing worked out when two people wanted different things.

Drew Dixon was a bull rider. She was a single mother. From what she could tell, he had nothing holding him back and making him settle down. She couldn't trust that she'd be the reason to make him stay when his injuries healed and the rodeo called his name. The rodeo was in his blood, and she wasn't the kind of woman to make a man choose her over the thing he loved the most.

It was best to walk away and avoid Drew Dixon completely than to allow herself the chance to believe things would be different and lose it all again. For both hers and Allie's sake.

CHAPTER FIFTEEN

Drew watched as Becca climbed into her car and pulled out of the drive. He had wanted to chase after her. He wanted to continue apologizing for getting too close, for pushing things too far. He hadn't meant to upset her, and judging by the way she'd looked at him, he'd done just that.

He released a slow breath as he made his way to the main house. He pulled open the screen door and kicked off his boots as he hung his hat on the hook by the door.

His mother rounded the corner and greeted him with a smile that quickly left when she realized he hadn't brought Becca inside with him.

"Where's Becca?"

Drew wasn't quite sure how to explain everything to his mother. Beverly Dixon was a woman who believed her sons were gentlemen, and with what had happened in the stalls... his mother might think differently of him. No matter how good of intentions he'd had. And he had only the best of intentions when it came to Becca. But none of that would matter when his mother found out Becca had left the ranch because of him.

"Is she out there?" Mama Dixon asked, looking around him in search of Becca. "Tell her to come on in. She doesn't need to be out there. We can all sit at the table and take a break."

"She's not here, Ma," Drew said, running a hand through his hair as he pulled up a chair at the table and sat down. He knocked his knuckles along the wood and waited for the realization to set in. His mother furrowed a brow and checked the front porch, not believing Becca had left.

She turned back toward him with a concerned look on her face. "Where'd she go?"

Drew fought the urge to play dumb, or to make something up. Instead, he told the truth, because at the end of the day, he was an honest man and what happened between them wasn't anyone's fault but his own.

"She went home, Ma," he said, straightening himself in the chair and preparing to explain. He hated to think that Becca would quit working at the ranch, or worse, stop bringing her daughter to riding lessons, because of him. But just in case she did, his mother deserved to know the truth. But even as he prepared himself to say the words, he couldn't. He'd seen the look in her eyes as he had leaned in to kiss her. He had felt the way she had leaned into him as their eyes locked in the moment.

"She—"

The crack of the screen door interrupted him as Blake rushed inside. "I need your help," he said, hooking a thumb over his shoulder. "It looks like your new horse got out of its pen and is headed toward the highway."

Drew couldn't explain the sudden rush of adrenaline he felt as he stood from the table. He left his mother's unanswered questions behind him as he stepped into his boots and grabbed his hat before rushing out the door.

The last thought he'd had before climbing into his truck with the trailer still hitched, was Becca driving home on the same highway the horse was headed for. His only hope was to find the horse before it got too far and caused an accident.

Blake climbed into the cab of the truck and slammed the door. "I don't think he's gotten too far. I figured I'd come along to help wrangle him into the trailer once Garrett ropes him."

Drew glanced over and saw Garrett riding Simon through the pasture and across their land in the direction Blake stated he'd seen the horse run off.

Drew pressed his foot against the gas pedal, praying they would find the horse before it wreaked havoc. He especially prayed the horse wouldn't cross paths with Becca on her way back into town. Her small car would be no match to a two-thousand-pound horse. There was no doubt in Drew's mind that the car would be totaled, and he didn't want to think about the possibility of Becca getting hurt.

"Hey, slow down a bit," Blake said. "We've got plenty of time to find him before it gets dark."

Drew gripped the steering wheel tighter. Finding the dark-colored horse at night was the least of his concern. "I'm not worried about that."

Blake tossed him a questioning glance before putting two and two together. "Oh."

They rode in silence along back roads while searching for the horse with no name. Drew guided the truck along the gravel roads, keeping his eye out for the untamed horse. He'd never once thought the horse would break free and make a run for it. He was proving to be more of a challenge than Drew had given him credit for. It had been foolish on Drew's part to believe he had what it would take to break the horse.

And now, because he'd been the one to bring it to the ranch, he'd put others in danger.

"Carolyn says Becca's home," Blake said in the seat next to him. Drew glanced over, taking one look at the screen on Blake's phone and realized his brother had texted Becca's mother. Drew released a sigh of relief as he steered the truck along the curved gravel roads. Blake set his phone down and pointed toward the speedometer on Drew's truck. "Mind slowing it down a notch or two now that we know she's safe?"

Drew did as his brother said, but he didn't slow down too much because they still had to worry about the horse making it to the highway. Their worry wasn't quite over until the horse was wrangled, back in the trailer, and on its way back to the ranch.

"I should've been more patient," Drew said, gripping the wheel and talking out loud. Blake rode along silently, looking in every direction for the horse. "If I had been more patient and willing to take things slower…"

He let his words trail off, knowing it didn't make any difference now.

"Are we still talking about the horse?"

Drew glanced over at his brother, who was no longer riding silently next to him. His brother was now asking questions that Drew wasn't sure he wanted to discuss with him right now.

"Why am I getting the feeling that you're no longer referring to the mistake of getting this horse?"

Drew tossed him a look that would tell him everything he wanted to know as he pulled the truck into a vacant drive leading to the middle of a field.

Garrett and Simon had caught up to the escapee and were doing their best to rope him when Drew shifted into park. With any luck at all, they would be able to wrangle the horse and have it back home on the ranch within the next half-hour, and Drew could avoid answering Blake's questions on the drive home.

"Bring him on over," Drew called out, motioning for Garrett to change direction. Garrett was good at roping, and from the look of it, had the horse roped within a few minutes.

Drew grabbed gloves out of his back pocket and slid them onto his hands. He'd managed to keep a spare pair in the glove box and had tossed them at Blake. "Let's hope he loads easier than he did the first time."

Drew shrugged, knowing he wouldn't be successful without his brother's help. Having one good arm meant he wouldn't be able to control the horse as well as he could if he'd had the strength and dominance of both arms. Thankfully, Blake knew how to handle the horse and guided him into the trailer.

"You made that look easy," Drew called out, wishing Blake would have been there to load the horse the first time.

"It's easy when you've been doing it a while," Blake shot back, offering a teasing grin. Drew tossed his head back and let out a laugh. "You're not wrong, but you're not right either."

He latched the trailer door and hollered a quick thanks to Garrett before climbing into the truck. He shifted the truck into gear and headed back down the gravel road.

He checked the mirrors, making sure the trailer was still intact and the horse was managing fine with the ride. The horse had managed just fine the first go around, so Drew didn't think there would be a problem this time. But with the way things were going…

"So, what happened between you and Becca?"

Drew tightened his grip on the steering wheel at the mention of Becca's name. The last thing he wanted to talk about, especially with his brother, was Becca.

"Nothing," he said, keeping it short and sweet. He didn't need his brother prying into his business, and he certainly didn't need any advice either.

Blake let out a chuckle and shook his head. The top of his cowboy hat grazed the ceiling of Drew's truck. The Dixon brothers were all around the same height, but Blake was an inch or two taller than Drew and Garrett. "Everything you've been saying up 'til now doesn't sound like nothing."

Drew kept his mouth quiet and his eyes on the road. He didn't want to give Blake the idea he was looking for conversation. He wouldn't give in to the prying questions either.

"It can't be that bad," Blake said. Drew knew he was doing everything in his power to make him spill the beans, but he wasn't going to. It wasn't any of his brother's business. Neither one of them, in fact. "I mean, aside from what they say about opposites attracting and all…"

Drew shot Blake a look, daring him to say another word. Blake raised his hands, and Drew shook his head. He couldn't be angry at Blake for trying to get information. They had all done it a time or two in the past. They were in their thirties, single, and it didn't help that their mother was harping on them to find the right woman and settle down. It also didn't help that their uncle Curt had threatened to bring Fran out to Montana to do a little matchmaking.

Drew didn't want to think about being matched with someone. He could manage well enough on his own. *But could he?*

The thought crossed his mind when he thought of Becca and trying to find love on his own. Heck, he hadn't even wanted to talk about love, let alone find it, and here he was…

"So you think you're taking things too fast?" Blake asked, prying once again and refusing to give it a rest. Drew blew out a breath and laughed. "Man, you just don't know when to give it up, do you?"

Blake shrugged and said, "I've learned from the best."

Drew tipped his head back and let out a laugh as he guided the truck down the driveway and parked it near the corral. Before they unloaded the horse, they would have to inspect the fence and find out how the darn thing managed its escape.

He killed the engine and tossed a look at Blake. "If I tell you, do you promise to keep quiet and not tell anybody?"

Drew wasn't sure why he'd make Blake promise. It wasn't like his brother would keep it anyway. The minute Drew wasn't within earshot, Blake would be blabbing his mouth to anyone who would listen. He couldn't blame him if he did, though, because he and Garrett had it coming from the last time Blake might have had an interest in someone and they'd blown it out of proportion.

Blake mocked Drew by holding up his pinky finger and laughed. "I pinky promise."

Drew slugged him in the shoulder and told him to get out the truck. They had work to do, and there wasn't time to waste talking about how foolish Drew had been.

"For what it's worth," Blake said, opening the passenger door and looking back as he stepped out, "if it's about that kiss the two of you shared in the barn... I'm pretty sure she likes you."

Before Drew had a chance to recover from the hit of Blake's words, and explain their lips hadn't even come close to meeting, Blake shut the door and tossed him a knowing grin. Drew ran a hand through his hair and wondered how in the world Blake had seen the two of them in the barn. He'd thought they were all alone. Just the two of them with Simon. How wrong he had been, and now he would never hear the end of it.

CHAPTER SIXTEEN

Becca stepped onto her mother's front porch and sat down in the wooden swing. The warmth from the summer sun skimmed her face as she took in the view around her, filled with children playing as mountains outlined the sky in the distance.

The view from town wasn't quite the same as it was in the country, but the feeling was all the same. She was back home for as long as she needed to be, and she felt comfort in knowing she and Allie would be taken care of by people who loved them no matter what.

She'd come back home without another choice. She had made the decision to move back home in order to get back on her feet without drowning.

Her thoughts drifted off to Chad, and she couldn't

help but wonder if there would come a time he would want Allie back in his life. How long it would take him to realize he still had a little girl who needed him.

It pained her to know the man she'd married had invested his time and his love into another woman, stepping completely out of bounds and breaking the vows they'd made on their wedding day.

She closed her eyes and willed her thoughts away. The last thing she wanted to think about was how devastated she had been the day she found out her marriage was over.

Her thoughts shifted from Chad to Drew, and she released a heavy sigh. Drew was everything her ex-husband wasn't. Where Chad had wanted to settle down and raise a family, Drew was flighty, unwilling to settle down, reckless and carefree.

But Drew was patient and gentle... kind to her daughter. He handled Becca's fears without judgment and took care to make her feel safe...

The thwack of the screen door pulled Becca out of her thoughts as her little girl rushed into her arms. "What are you doing out here, Mama?"

"Hey, baby." Becca smiled and pulled her daughter into her lap. She wrapped her arms tightly around Allie and kissed her head. "I just needed a minute to enjoy the fresh air," she said, looking into her daughter's bright blue eyes. Her daughter had the grace of God, and she couldn't thank the good Lord enough for allowing her to be Allie's mother. "Did you get a lot of baking done?"

"Uh huh," Allie said, nodding her head slowly. She slid off of Becca's lap and tugged on her hand as she tried to pull her off the swing. "Come and look, Mama."

Becca stood from the swing and allowed her daughter to lead her into the house. As they stepped inside, Becca kicked off her sandals. She could smell the peanut butter wafting from the kitchen as they neared the dining room and rounded the corner. She smiled as her mother placed cookies on the cooling racks lining the countertops.

"See, Mama," Allie said, climbing onto a bar stool near the counter and leaning over her prized possessions.

Becca smiled as she tucked a curl behind her daughter's ear and slid onto the chair next to her. "It looks like you and Nana were busy today."

Allie nodded proudly and said, "Nana loves baking with me. She says I'm the best cookie smasher."

Becca raised a brow and turned to her mother, who was placing the last of the baked cookies onto a nearby rack. "Cookie smasher?" she questioned, taking a look at the cookies with a playful expression on her face. "These cookies don't look too smashed to me."

Allie giggled next to her as she shook her head. "No, Mama," she said through the giggles. "Look."

Allie pointed to the middle of a peanut butter cookie where a milk chocolate star had been pressed. "I smashed the cookie to make room for the chocolate."

Becca listened intently over the next few minutes as her daughter demonstrated the process of pressing chocolate stars into the center of the cookies. As Becca listened, she tried to sneak a cookie from a nearby rack and caught a side-eye from Allie. Allie shook her head and waved a finger back and forth in front of her. "Not yet. They have to cool."

"Ah, I see," Becca said with a knowing smile. It was her mother's way of keeping tiny fingers off the cookies once they were placed to cool. A way of keeping the Cookie Monster from eating them all before they made it to the cookie jar. "Well, then, I suppose I'll just have to eat one after supper."

Allie went about her business, tending to the chocolate stars and pressing them firmly into place as Becca leaned back and relaxed.

Allie slid off the chair a minute later and rounded the kitchen counter. Becca watched as her daughter grabbed a baggy full of cookies from the shelf and brought them over to her. "We even made cookies for Drew," she said proudly, holding up the bag in front of Becca. Becca looked from the cookies to her mother, who was now busying herself with clean up duties and avoiding Becca's questioning glances. "Do you think he'll like them, Mama?"

Becca righted her expression and smiled at her beautiful daughter. "I'm sure he will, baby."

"Good," her daughter said, placing them on the counter and looking back at her grandmother. "We even made some for everyone else."

"That's very thoughtful of you," Becca said, running a hand through her daughter's curls and wondering how she got so lucky to have such an amazing little girl. "I'm sure everyone will enjoy the cookies a little bit more just knowing they came from you and Nana."

"That's what Nana said," Allie confirmed, swiping a cookie off the rack and taking a bite. Becca furrowed a playful brow and tickled her Cookie Monster. Allie quickly grabbed a cookie for Becca and waited for her to try it. Becca took a bite and allowed the chocolate to melt in her mouth. There was no doubt that peanut butter cookies were still her favorite. The added chocolate star on top was a bonus. "These are so good."

"Thank you," Allie answered proudly with a mouthful of cookie.

Carolyn rounded the corner and took a vacant spot next to them. Becca smiled at her mother while finishing off the last bite of her cookie and thanked her for baking with Allie. From the looks of it, the two of them made a wonderful team when it came to baking, and several people around town would be enjoying cookies made with lots of love.

"Did you have a good day at the ranch, Mama?"

Becca glanced over at her mother before answering the question. "I did."

She wasn't sure if she would offer much about her day. Aside from helping Mama Dixon with the dishes and taking lunch out to Drew, Becca hadn't done much else.

Her mind drifted off to the moment they'd shared in the barn. The rush of butterflies it had given her to stand so close to him. How safe she'd felt standing beside him as she came face to face with Simon. The warmth of his breath on her face as they leaned into one another… and his lips close enough to kiss…

"Do you like horses now, Mama?"

Allie's question pulled Becca out of her thoughts, and her mother tossed her a knowing smile. Becca could tell her mother had questions of her own but was waiting for a better time to ask them. She wasn't quite sure what she would tell her mother—if anything at all.

The moment she'd shared with Drew had been nothing but… *what*?

"I, um," Becca struggled to find the right answer for her daughter. Did she tell Allie that she'd spent time with Simon and Drew? Did she play it off and pretend the only thing she did was help around the kitchen? She wasn't quite sure how much she wanted to tell. Not because she didn't want her daughter to know. It wasn't that at all. It was the fact she didn't want her daughter to get her hopes up. If her daughter knew she had spent time with Simon, Allie would assume her mom's fears were gone and she'd spend time next to Allie during riding lessons.

"I haven't decided yet," Becca said with a smile. Playing it safe would be her best bet. "Simon seems like a really good horse, though."

Becca's mother shot her a knowing look and a smile. Becca ignored it as Allie continued asking questions.

"Did Drew take you to meet Simon?"

Becca could feel her mother's questioning eyes on her. She had no choice but to be honest with Allie, and she would later explain to her mother that regardless of what she believed, there could never be anything between her and Drew Dixon.

"He did," Becca answered honestly, ignoring her mother's expression from the corner of her eye and continuing her conversation with Allie.

"So do you like him now, Mama?"

Allie's eyes lit up with her question as she leaned into Becca's lap. Becca hesitated a minute before answering the question, feeling the weight of honesty creeping in. Even though her daughter was asking about whether Becca liked the horse, her thoughts went straight to Drew. He had become the sole operator of her thoughts, and Becca wasn't liking the effect he'd had on her. The fear she'd had of horses seemed miniscule compared to the fear she now had of Drew.

Not because he was a bad guy, but solely because he not only stole her daughter's heart, but he was stealing Becca's as well.

The fear of that realization set in, and Becca knew she was in trouble. There were several reasons for her not to fall in love with Drew Dixon. More than a few reasons she could tick off in under a minute with the first one being that he wasn't planning to stay in Woodford Creek.

When Becca hadn't answered Allie, her mother stepped into the conversation and suggested Allie take a few cookies over to her friend, Rosie, and play for a bit before suppertime.

"Love you, Mama," Allie called out as she raced toward the front door with a handful of cookies and a wide smile on her face.

"Love you, too, baby," Becca called out over her shoulder and turned toward her mother. She placed her head in her hands and thanked her mother for giving her an out, all while knowing she would have questions of her own. Thankfully, though, her mother wouldn't pry, and she would patiently wait for Becca to be the first to open up.

Becca released a sigh and combed a hand through her hair. She hadn't meant for anything to happen between her and Drew. She'd wanted to keep her distance, look after Allie from afar while she rode in the saddle. She'd had it all planned out...

"Want to talk about it?"

Becca met her mother's concerned eyes with her own and thought about it for a minute. Ever since she was a little girl, she'd confided in her mother about everything. There wasn't a single thing Becca had kept from her mother. Their relationship strengthened over time, and after the rollercoaster of Becca's teenage years and her parents' divorce, the two of them were more than mother and daughter—they were best friends.

"I'm not sure there's much to talk about," Becca said, wondering what good it would do to talk about it anyway. There was no telling what would happen when Becca returned to the ranch. It wasn't like she could truly avoid Drew now that she worked there, and she had a feeling things would be awkward for a while, too.

Her mother pushed off the counter and walked over to the cupboard. She glanced over her shoulder at Becca and asked, "Would you like some tea?"

Becca nodded and gladly accepted the glass as her mother slid it in front of her. "Thanks."

"I'm not sure what happened today, but I know that whatever happened has you distracted and consumed by your thoughts," her mother stated matter-of-factly. Becca couldn't argue with her. Her mother knew her better than anyone else, and to say otherwise would be lying.

"Things might have gone completely unexpected between us," Becca said, taking a drink before setting her glass down. She wrapped her hands around the glass and focused on the floating ice cubes. "I hadn't planned on getting close to him…"

Her words trailed off as she thought of how best to explain what happened between them. There really was no explanation. It just happened.

"I know you're hurting and wanting to take your time," her mother said, reaching out and grabbing a hold of Becca's hand. The same as Drew had when she'd talked about her past. "But I don't think you have anything to worry about when it comes to Drew."

Becca traced the rim of the glass with her thumb as she thought about what her mother was saying. Becca wasn't wanting to jump into a relationship so soon after walking away from a failed marriage. The last thing she wanted was to rush things with Drew and risk her daughter getting hurt in the process.

"He's just everything I'm not," Becca said with a sigh. "Not to mention, I shouldn't be falling head over heels for a man so soon after a failed marriage. I should be taking my time and—"

"You're not doing anything wrong, dear," her mother assured her, offering her hand a gentle squeeze. "Sometimes love comes when we least expect it, and sometimes we question things when we should just go along with them."

Becca thought about her mother's words for a minute. Hesitation and doubt filled her thoughts when she realized her mother might be right.

"I know I haven't talked a lot about my divorce from your father," her mother started, checking over her shoulder at the sound of little feet. Allie grabbed a doll from the dining room and headed back outside. Her mother turned back to her and said, "It was hard at first. Starting over and figuring out life on my own."

Becca silently nodded, listening intently to her mother explain how she overcame the divorce neither of them saw coming. Becca knew it hadn't been easy for her mother. She recalled memories of life soon after her parents' divorce, and she remembered the pain and unanswered questions.

"I had so much to think about," her mother continued. "There was you, where we would live, and how I would make it on my own."

Becca silently nodded along as she listened. Her mother might have mentioned a thing or two about her divorce through the years, but until now, it hadn't made much sense. Only now, Becca could relate to her mother's story, along with all the fears and worries she'd had along the way.

"But I was mostly worried about you," her mother stated, offering Becca a half-smile. "I wanted to make sure you were well taken care of no matter what, and to know you were loved. Much like you with Allie."

Becca felt the sting of tears in her eyes and willed them away. She understood where her mother was going with this, and she didn't want to cry. Not today. She'd done enough crying over the last few months.

"There was a point when I quit worrying so much and ended up doing the best I could, because I knew at the end of the day, I loved you enough for the both of us and I would do whatever it took to make sure you and I were okay."

Becca wiped a stray tear from her cheek and smiled at her mother. The love her mother had for her was beyond unconditional, and Becca would be forever thankful for the loving relationship they shared.

"I guess what I'm trying to say is," her mother paused, taking a moment to gather her thoughts into words, "you can't stop living life because you're scared. Fear is the devil's work, and no one said life after divorce would be easy. But no one said it had to be difficult, either. There are no rules to love, and as long as you feel it's right in your heart, Becca, you've got to follow it and allow those who care about you in."

Her mother's words resonated deeply within her as she thought about the time they'd spent with Drew. He'd shown them nothing but the best, and Becca had no reason to doubt him, regardless of the fear she felt about him leaving them behind when his injured arm healed. Regardless of what happened, she couldn't live in fear and drown in worry.

"Drew might be a little rough around the edges, but from what I've seen and heard, he cares about you and Allie," her mother stated matter-of-factly. Becca wanted to ask her what she was supposed to do. How she was supposed to move forward when the hurt of her past was weighing so heavily on her heart. She couldn't push through the damage Chad had done on her own.

"I don't think I'm strong enough to get through this," she whispered with tears welling in her eyes and threatening their escape. She held back as the lump of emotion formed in her throat. She'd never been one to talk about her weakness, but in that moment, sitting right there next to her mother, she had no choice. She needed to talk about it and get everything off of her chest. "I don't think I can make it on my own, Mama."

Her mother squeezed her hand and offered a tearful smile. "But you are, Bec," she softly whispered through the emotion in voice. "You're doing exactly what you think you can't. You're going to get through this, and I'm right here to make sure of it. You don't have to worry about making it on your own, because you have me. You have people who love you and will take care of you and Allie, Bec."

Becca felt the tears stream down her face as she listened to what her mother was saying. She had no reason to worry. No reason to fear what was coming. She didn't need to worry about tomorrow while focusing on today.

"You have people who will take care of you and Allie if you're willing to let them."

Becca hung on every word her mother was saying. She knew deep down her mother was right. There was no doubt about it. Her heart ached at the thought of everything she'd lost with Chad, but she couldn't dwell on that. She needed to let go and move forward. She had a newfound hope. Everything would be okay. She just needed to take things one day at a time.

CHAPTER SEVENTEEN

Drew watched as Allie scrambled out of the backseat of her grandmother's car and headed straight toward him and the new horse.

"Whoa, there little buddy," he called out, motioning for her to slow down. "We've got a new horse, and he spooks a little easier than Simon. So I need you to take small, slow steps, okay?"

Allie nodded as she looked past Drew, checking out the new horse behind him. He'd decided to work with the horse after lunch since he'd spent most of the morning mucking the stalls. Drew had planned to be right where he was standing when Allie showed up, so he'd timed it just right as he stared down at the curly blonde in front of him. "Is that your new horse?"

"Yep," Drew said, moving to the side so Allie could get a better look. "I need you to promise me that you'll keep your distance, okay?"

Again, Allie offered a nod as she watched the horse in awe. "Is he wild?"

Drew laughed. "Well, some would like to think so, but I'm willing to change their minds."

Allie's face lit up with a smile that met her eyes. "When can I ride him?"

"Not for a while," Drew said, turning around when he heard footsteps behind them. Carolyn approached him with a friendly wave and a kind smile. He gave the woman his full attention. "Good afternoon, ma'am."

"None of that," she scolded. "Just call me Carolyn. But yes, it's a good afternoon. Allie couldn't wait to get to her riding lessons. She's been talking about Simon since she got up this morning."

Drew looked down at Allie who nodded without hesitation.

"Uh huh," she said. "I missed you guys."

Drew thought his heart might have skipped a beat or two when Allie's sweet words hit him. Whew, he was becoming a softy nowadays. "Well, we've missed you, too."

"Well, as long as you two are good, I think I'm going to pay a visit to Bev and say hello to my daughter while I'm at it."

Carolyn reached for Allie and wrapped her arms tightly around the little girl. "You have fun with Drew today and be on your best behavior, okay?"

Allie nodded, offering her grandmother a quick peck on the cheek. "I'm always good, Nana."

Drew met Carolyn's eyes and went along with Allie. The young girl behaved better than most kids her age, and he gave Becca credit for that.

"Okay, well then, I'll see you later, Allie-gator," Carolyn said, giving her granddaughter a quick kiss.

"Afterwhile, crocodile," Allie sang out as she stood beside him and waved to her grandmother.

"In an hour, sunflower," Carolyn called out over her shoulder.

"Maybe two, kangaroo," Allie said, giggling.

"Gotta go, buffalo," Carolyn called back with a quick wave of her hand.

Drew listened as the two of them carried on and wondered where they'd gotten that from, deciding it must have been something Allie had learned in school.

When Carolyn had made it to the house, Allie turned to him and said, "I love her so much."

Drew tipped his hat to block the afternoon sun from his eyes as he looked down at Allie. "She is pretty great, isn't she?"

"Yep, she sure is."

"What do you say we get to work on some riding

lessons?" Drew asked, hitching a thumb over his shoulder toward the stables. Simon would be ready and waiting for them to come and get him out for the day. Drew had spent most of the morning mucking the stalls, cleaning the place up while keeping his mind off the beautiful brunette that was in the house with his mother. "I'm sure Simon would love to see you."

Allie kicked up her feet and hightailed it to the stables. "Last one there's a rotten egg," she called over her shoulder in a fit of laughter.

Drew made a mad dash for the stables. He couldn't be beat by a six-year-old, could he?

Sure enough, he could.

"You're the rotten egg," Allie sang out, dancing in a circle and pointing at him.

"I'm not rotten," he teased. "I let you win."

Allie rolled her eyes with a laugh and said, "Whatever."

She was right though. He was last, he was the rotten egg, and he was winded. There was no way she'd ever believe he hadn't tried to beat her to the stables. He was too out of shape to race a small child —that much he knew now. Maybe they'd make it a daily thing and he'd be able to beat her at least once.

Drew shrugged off his loss and high-fived Allie. He pushed open the door and followed Allie inside.

The stalls were filled with fresh hay, and Drew was happy he'd made it a priority first thing today.

"What do you say we take Simon on a ride down by the creek again?" Drew asked as they approached Simon's stall. He readied the horse, opening the stall door and allowing Simon to walk out. Allie stayed beside Drew, listening intently to his instructions as he helped her into the saddle. He'd done the best he could one-handed, and to be honest, he thought he'd done fairly well. There were things he couldn't do, like hold his own when it came to the new horse, but other than that, he had operating one-handed down pat.

"When we get back, maybe we can find some ice cream and give the new horse a name," Drew offered, leading Simon and Allie out of the stables and onto the path toward the creek. "I was thinking about letting you name him because I'm not too good with names. You can even ask Simon. He'll be the first to tell you."

Allie chuckled as she held tightly to the reins and guided Simon along the well-worn path. Flowers lined both sides of the path, and Drew wondered what Becca would do if they brought her flowers. He'd make sure Simon didn't eat them this time.

"I like Simon's name, though," Allie answered honestly, and Drew thanked her. Even today, he wasn't too sure how he'd come up with the name for the horse.

"Well, I think he's happy to hear that," Drew teased and continued walking along with Allie and Simon. He allowed them to get a few feet in front of him, giving Allie a little leeway to control the horse on her own and find comfort in knowing she could.

Drew bent down and plucked a few wildflowers from the field and held them close. He wouldn't let Simon eat them before getting them back to Becca. He'd thought about the time the two of them had shared, and he couldn't shake the thoughts of what happened in the stables.

"There's the creek," Allie said, pulling Drew out of his thoughts. He jogged a little ways to catch up to them and steadied Simon by the reins as Allie climbed down. "Can I walk in the water?"

Drew held tightly to Simon's reins and thought about it for a minute. He didn't see what walking in the creek would hurt, but he didn't know whether or not Becca would be okay with it.

"I'm not sure it's a good idea without asking your mother first," he said, releasing Simon's reins and approaching Allie's side. She stood at the edge of the creek and kicked off her shoes.

"Now you sound like my dad," Allie said. Her tone caught Drew off guard. He wasn't exactly sure how to respond to that. He didn't know much about the girl's father, and it wasn't his place to question anything in regard to that situation. "He used to tell me it was up to mom *all* the time."

Drew paid attention to what Allie wasn't saying. He could hear the emotion in her voice as she talked about her father, and he couldn't help but wonder if the man Becca had been married to had anything to do with Allie now that things were over.

He looked down at his hands, hanging onto the flowers he'd picked for Becca. Allie turned to face him, and he wasn't sure what he would say to the girl if she started asking him questions, or worse, told him about her parents. To say it would be awkward was an understatement.

"Do you like my mom?"

Allie's question hit him like a ton of bricks. He should have seen it coming, but he'd been blindsided to say the least. Now, he fought to find the words he'd say and would struggle in telling the girl about his feelings not only for Becca, but for Allie as well.

How could he put everything he felt into words? He couldn't explain it to himself, let alone to a six-year-old.

"Well, I…"

Allie glanced down at his hands holding the flowers and looked up at him. "Are those for my mom?"

He let out a half-laugh and gripped the back of his

neck with his free hand. He wasn't one to get embarrassed or thrown off in the slightest, but the girl standing in front of him had managed to do just that.

"It's okay if you like her," Allie said, offering a slight shrug. "I think she likes you, too."

Drew tipped his head to the side and raised a brow. "Why do you think that?"

Allie picked up a rock and skipped it into the creek. She offered a slight shrug and said, "I heard her talking to Nana about you. I think she's worried you're going to make her sad like my daddy did."

Allie's words hit him square in the chest. He wasn't too sure he knew what to say in response to that tidbit of information, but he wanted Allie to know his intentions were better than that. But at the same time, he figured it was best to leave well enough alone and call it a day before riding back to the house.

He shook off the effect of Allie's words and righted himself next to Simon. He watched as the young girl tossed a few more rocks into the creek before he cleared his throat and asked, "What do you say we get ourselves some ice cream?"

With that, Allie left the creek behind and headed for Simon. "And name your new horse, too?"

And just like that, the conversation about Becca had changed direction and Drew thanked the good Lord. He would leave any explaining about the two of them to Becca. He had no right telling Allie about his intentions and how he felt about her and her mother.

"Yeah, I suppose we could eat ice cream at the picnic table under the willow and talk about what to name him," Drew said, climbing up into the saddle behind Allie. "But we've gotta get there first."

With that, he made sure Allie had a hold on the reins and gave Simon a gentle but firm squeeze to get him to move as he held onto the flowers he'd picked for Becca.

Only after they'd put Simon away did they head into the main house. Allie called out for her mother while Drew followed her into the kitchen from the porch.

They found the three women gathered around the kitchen table. All eyes were on them as they entered the room, and Drew looked down at the flowers he'd forgotten all about until just now. He'd picked them for Becca, but now that their mothers were gathered around, he felt a bit uneasy about handing them to her.

"Look what Drew picked for you, Mama," Allie called out, pulling Drew along behind her. "He even made sure Simon didn't eat them this time."

Becca's eyes focused on him as he neared the table. He held the flowers up with a nervous smile on his face and prayed like crazy that she wouldn't think he'd lost his mind.

"Aww, now isn't that just the sweetest thing," Carolyn said, nudging her daughter in the arm as she glanced between the two of them. His mother sat back with a warm smile as the pieces fell together in front of her. He'd known his mother had a feeling about him and Becca, but at first, he'd called her bluff. Now, however, he realized she'd been right all along.

"What do you say we grab some ice cream, Allie?" his mother asked, leaving the table along with Carolyn as they headed for the freezer. Becca stayed put, her eyes focused on him and the flowers he'd picked just for her. He couldn't tell what she was thinking, but judging by the look on her face, she was just as surprised as their mothers had been.

"Thank you," she whispered softly, accepting the flowers and bringing them close enough to smell. "You didn't have—"

"He likes you, Mama," Allie called out from the edge of the counter as she ate her ice cream. Drew wondered if it was the right time to mention their plan of eating ice cream under the willow and naming the horse.

There was no better time than now, as their mothers crowded around them, to make a move and free them from the thousand questions to follow.

"What do you say we head out to the willow tree and get to naming that horse out there?" Drew asked, throwing a look over his shoulder. "Isn't that what we'd planned to do once we got our ice cream?"

Allie jumped off the chair and grabbed her ice cream cone before racing him out the door. He was more than happy to see Becca following them outside.

He held the door open for her, leaving their mothers in the kitchen to talk about what might be transpiring between the two of them, and smiled when Becca gave him a look that told him that he might be in trouble.

CHAPTER EIGHTEEN

"What's all this about?"

She followed Drew out onto the front porch, leaving her mother and Mama Dixon in the kitchen. Of course, they were chatty Cathys about what was happening with her and Drew. She could tell just by the sly grins on their faces right before she'd left the kitchen.

"What?" Drew spun around and faced her, his lips pulling into one of those all-too-familiar grins. If she looked closely enough, she would have sworn she could see sparks of mischief firing in his eyes.

"You know what," she playfully scolded, tossing a look over her shoulder and wondering if their mothers were still watching from afar. She didn't have a clear view of the table from where she was standing, but there was no doubt in her mind that they were cemented in their seats watching with hopeful hearts.

Drew's soft brown eyes, along with his dimple-filled smile, were too much for her. She couldn't even pretend to be upset while standing face to face with him.

He offered a light shrug and took a step closer. He reached out, offering for her to take his hand. She glanced over his shoulder, checking to make sure Allie was nowhere near the new horse. Instead, she was off playing on the tire swing while finishing her ice cream. Becca had thought Drew wanted to meet under the willow tree to discuss what to name the horse. She was surprised to find herself placing her hand into Drew's.

"So you didn't like the flowers?" he asked, staring into her eyes. She tried hard to concentrate on what he'd asked, but she found it overwhelmingly difficult.

"I liked them," Becca admitted. She enjoyed receiving flowers every now and then. It made her feel loved. And the flowers she received today were extra special because, aside from being some of her favorite wildflowers, they were picked especially for her by Drew. That alone made her heart swell and the butterflies come to life. "I just…"

She looked down at their hands. His hand gently held onto hers as they stood less than a few inches apart on the Dixons's front porch. She looked back up at him, wanting to tell him everything she'd been meaning to, but not quite sure how to put her feelings into words. Her mother had told her to take it one day at a time, but standing there in the moment with Drew in front of her... That advice seemed easier said than done.

He pulled her close, closing the distance between them. She waited with bated breath as he looked down at her, focusing on her lips. She couldn't breathe while knowing what was about to happen. She wanted him to kiss her, but at the same time, she wanted to run and hide. Becca couldn't deny the feelings were stronger than she'd ever felt before.

Her thoughts battled for priority. She fought between pulling away and giving in. Preventing this rush of emotion and allowing herself the chance to feel what she so desperately wanted to feel. To give Drew the chance to prove he wouldn't break her heart and leave her wishing she never would have...

He leaned in, his breath warm on her nose as she stared up at him before closing her eyes. She counted the seconds that passed until she felt his lips on hers. She fought the urge to run, and instead, decided to stay wrapped in his arms.

A soft breeze blew through Becca's hair, drawing her further into the moment with Drew and causing her heart to race as she melted into his embrace.

Clapping from inside the house interrupted their

moment, causing them to turn and face their mothers who were now pressed against the screen door with grins wider than Montana on their face.

Becca released the breath she'd been holding as she shyly ran a hand through her hair. She couldn't believe she'd gotten lost in the moment. She'd been carried away and made to forget everything around her for just a fraction of a minute.

"Mama, are you two coming or not?" Allie called out from the bottom of the steps. Becca had been so caught up in the kiss, standing in Drew's arms, that she hadn't realized her daughter had left the swing to meet them on the porch. "I've already finished my ice cream."

Becca tucked a loose strand of hair behind her daughter's ear and assured her there was plenty of time to name the horse. She glanced over her shoulder, wondering just how long her mother and Mama Dixon had been standing at the door watching such an intimate moment. And her daughter… how long had Allie been standing at the bottom of the stairs without saying a word. How much had she seen?

"Told you she likes you," Allie said, making her way up the steps and over to the wooden swing. Becca looked from her daughter to Drew and wondered what on earth her daughter was talking about.

Drew offered a subtle shrug and said, "She

might've overheard a conversation you might have had with your mother."

Becca shot a questioning look at Allie, who in return offered a look of innocence. She had tried so hard to keep things out of earshot, but she must have allowed a bit too much slip out without realizing Allie had been nearby.

She would have a talk with Allie later, after supper and bathtime. She would tuck her daughter in and take a few extra minutes not only to discuss what Allie might have overheard, but also her feelings about Becca and Drew.

"Well, at least now they have something to talk about," Drew said, pulling Becca's attention from the wooden swing back to the door. Her mother and Mama Dixon were nowhere in sight, and she could only imagine what had gone through their minds as they witnessed Becca and Drew's first kiss.

What had gone through Becca's?

"Let's go," Allie said, tugging at Becca's hand and pulling her toward the steps. Becca tossed a glance at Drew and pulled him along. If she was needing to go somewhere, he needed to come along too.

"Where are we going?" Becca asked, keeping up with her daughter as she followed her down the porch steps and out toward the pasture where the lone horse galloped in circles.

"To meet the horse I'm going to name," Allie said with a bright, wide smile as she motioned for Becca and Drew to hurry up.

Becca tossed a look at Drew, knowing it had been his idea for Allie to name the horse. She couldn't thank him enough for allowing her daughter the chance to do something like that. She was certain it would be something Allie would never forget.

Drew offered one of his notorious grins and subtle shrugs as they neared the corral. Drew called out to Allie, "Remember what I told you earlier?"

Allie stopped near the gate and turned to face Drew. Becca watched the interaction between Drew and her daughter, finding comfort in the way they'd bonded. If she hadn't known any better, one would think Drew was Allie's father.

"But can I pet him now?"

Allie's question was full of concern as she looked from Drew back to the horse. Becca wasn't so sure she wanted Allie around the animal, but was certain Drew wouldn't let her. Not when he was just getting started with the horse himself.

"I'll tell you what," Drew said, kneeling down in front of Allie and lifting her chin with his finger. Allie's smile had turned into a frown once she realized she wouldn't be able to see the horse up close. But leave it to Drew to make things better; that's exactly what he was getting ready to do. Becca leaned back and watched in silence. "I'll get him over here, and maybe he'll let you pet him."

Drew tossed a look at Becca, and she knew that he was asking her if it was all right for him to lift Allie at the gate. Becca nodded with a smile, thankful he had the respect to ask her first. Maybe her mother had been right all along about him.

"Okay, ready?" Drew asked, preparing Allie to climb her way onto the railing as they waited for the horse to make his rounds. Becca stood behind them, anticipating the interaction between the wild animal and her daughter. She prayed the horse wouldn't spook and go crazy with her daughter and Drew close enough to hurt them. "Here he comes. Hold your hand out nice and easy like this," Drew said, holding his hand out and showing Allie just how to do it when the horse approached them. At first, Becca could see the hesitation in the horse's posture. The way the horse paused just before the gate and took in his surroundings, making sure it was safe to approach. She found it silly that she could relate to the horse in that exact moment. She'd been afraid to commit. Afraid to allow others near her, and more than afraid to allow them in. She'd built up a wall to protect her heart, knowing the pieces she'd glued back together were more than fragile.

The horse slowly greeted Allie and Drew, taking a minute to sniff their hands before closing the distance between them with only the gate separating them.

Becca watched in silence as Allie gently stroked the horse's snout. She waited with stilled breathing as Drew and Allie offered the horse a sense of security. There was something about the way Drew stood against the railing that caught her attention. He stood broad shouldered and confident, yet he radiated a gentleness and a patience she'd never seen before.

"Thatta boy," Drew said, his voice low and his tone soft. He patted the horse's neck one last time before the horse had had enough and trotted away. Becca let out a slow breath, thankful that nothing horrible had happened. She was slowly warming up to horses, but it would take some time for her to fully trust again.

"He's coming around," Drew said proudly as he turned back to Becca and smiled. "Did you see that?"

Becca nodded and wrapped her arms around Allie as she pulled her in close. Allie loved the horses more than anything, and for her sake, Becca was thankful the horse had allowed her to pet him.

"Can I still name him?" Allie asked from Becca's side.

Drew looked from Becca to Allie and said, "Of course. What name are you thinking about giving him?"

"Chance."

"Chance, huh?"

Becca and Drew shared a glance before asking why Allie had chosen that name, though Becca had a feeling she knew why before her daughter said, "Because. You're giving him a chance to be the best horse he can be, and he's giving you a chance to love him."

Becca watched Drew take in her daughter's explanation and felt proud to be her mother. Allie had a way of breaking things down and making sense out of everything. From making new friends, to including everyone, all the way to understanding the makings of a good horse.

"That name fits him well, baby," Becca said with a smile. She was truly proud of her daughter for coming up with such a solid-fitting name. And not to mention her reasoning behind giving the horse that name to begin with.

"Rightfully so," Drew said, smiling down at Allie as he stepped closer to Becca. "I think it's a good name, and like your mother said, it fits him well."

Allie smiled from ear to ear and took off toward the house. Becca called after her, wondering where she was going in such a hurry. Of course, Allie wanted to share the new name she'd chosen with her grandmother and Mama Dixon.

"Well, there's that," Drew said, slapping his hands against his pant legs. Becca ran a hand through her wind-blown waves and gathered her hair at the nape of her neck.

"What would you say if I asked you to dinner tonight?"

"Tonight?" Becca questioned, thrown completely off guard.

"Yes, tonight," Drew confirmed. "You and Allie with me and the Dixon bunch."

He let out a light chuckle, and Becca had to wonder if he was being serious. She wanted to say yes, but at the same time…

"I don't think I can," she blurted without thinking it through. He would ask her why she couldn't, and she'd be without a response. She silently kicked herself. "I mean, I can, but…"

He raised a brow and stepped back, giving her a minute to collect her thoughts. She took a full minute before saying, "I think I need to talk with Allie first. Let her know what's going on…"

Drew's eyes landed on hers, and in that moment she forgot what she was saying. "I'm pretty sure she already knows."

Becca slowly nodded and debated on whether or not to tell Drew everything. She'd only mentioned a few things here and there, but if he was going to be a part of their lives, he had a right to know. And he needed to know that dealing with a six-year-old wasn't always smooth sailing. Some days were harder than others, especially if she was overwhelmed by thoughts of her father that made her miss him.

"Allie and I have a special relationship," Becca explained. "I don't like to hide anything from her. And I—"

"Bec," he said, cutting her off as he stepped closer. "I didn't mean it in a bad way. I just meant that she's smart and she's caught onto a lot of things that have been happening lately."

Becca sighed. "That's what I'm afraid of. I haven't had a chance to talk with her about everything," Becca explained, feeling the guilt pressing down. "There's a lot that she's still processing when it comes to her father. I don't want her to think that I'm keeping her away from him."

Drew remained quiet, listening to Becca explain how she truly felt. It felt good to finally be able to say it out loud.

"Things went from good to bad in such a short time, and now we're here," Becca said, fanning her arms at her side. "And now there's you…"

Her words trailed off, and she realized Drew hadn't taken his eyes off her once. "I just don't want to rush things. I need time. Time to explain things to Allie. Time to feel what I need to feel without worrying I'm making the wrong choice."

Drew straightened in front of her and nodded. He removed his hat from his head and ran a steady hand through his hair. Becca couldn't imagine what was going through his mind. She could only hope he understood where she was coming from.

"I have more than just myself to think about, Drew," Becca said, taking a step back. "I just need to take things slow, okay? Just one day at a time."

"I'm more than okay with that, Bec," Drew said, his eyes focused on hers. "Trust me. I might be a lot of things, but I'm not a jerk. I get it."

She couldn't argue with him. She felt the weight of the world lift off of her shoulders when she expressed her feelings and he responded so receptively.

"Trust me, Bec. The last thing I want is to hurt you or Allie."

Becca nodded, knowing his words were sincere and full of promise. She wanted to believe him. She would have given everything to fully trust in every word he'd said, but she couldn't. She'd been down this road once before. With a man who had promised her the world in one breath, and took it all away in the next.

Things were moving too fast with her and Drew. It was time to slow them down.

"I'll see you tomorrow?" Becca asked, waiting for him to respond before telling him goodbye and heading back to the house. She would grab Allie and head for home. Then she would make it a point to have the much-needed conversation with Allie tonight after her bath and make sure she was okay with the possibility of Becca's new relationship.

She took her time walking to the house. She tried her hardest to get her thoughts in order and prepare herself for the twenty questions from the two women who would be waiting for her inside.

There wasn't much to say other than the fact she was thankful Drew had given her a chance to tell him how she felt. She was even more thankful that he was willing to slow things down. That meant more to her than anything. Just knowing he was there for her and was giving her what she needed most.

Deep down it felt like a weight had been lifted, but she still felt horrible about turning down his invitation to dinner.

CHAPTER NINETEEN

Drew had spent the evening, late into the night, working with Chance after Becca and Allie had gone home. He had high hopes the horse would come around and be another great workhorse at the Dixon Ranch.

Mainly, though, he had worked to keep his thoughts occupied and off Becca. He couldn't believe she had turned down dinner, but then again, he would have too if it meant eating with his brothers.

But today was a new day, and he had a few things to mark off the list before lunchtime. He gathered his training rope from the stable and headed out in search of Chance, walking by Simon on his way out and promising the horse he'd be back after a while.

The thought of Allie and her grandmother's banter from the day before brought a smile to his face as the urge to add to his own remark by saying "see ya later, alligator" came to mind. But he refrained. He would just have to remember to try it out when Allie came back for her riding lesson.

Drew walked out of the stables and headed toward the pasture. He'd planned on guiding Chance in and hopefully get him into the corral without much fight.

To his surprise, the horse was ready and waiting for him as Drew approached him. The horse didn't move a muscle and allowed Drew to place a rope around him and guide him.

"Well, look at that," Becca said, keeping her distance. She was standing near the edge of the pasture in a soft blue-and-white striped sundress with her brown hair falling on her shoulders in waves. Drew really hadn't ever seen a woman as beautiful as Becca.

"He's definitely making progress," Drew stated, leading Chance out of the pasture. He hesitated a minute before leading him too far. He wanted to make sure Becca was okay with Chance before he went any further. As though she read his thoughts, she nodded and motioned for him to bring the horse out.

"Nice and easy," Drew said, keeping his tone light as he guided the horse. To his surprise, Becca stood off to the side, patiently waiting with an outstretched hand. Drew smiled and brought Chance over to her. He stood between them, making sure nothing would happen to cause either of them to startle.

Becca smiled when Chance nudged her with his nose. "Wow," she said with a bright smile on her face. Her eyes lit up, and for a minute, Drew didn't see a sign of fear on her face.

"I think he likes you," Drew said. "Want to walk with us to the corral?"

Becca glanced back toward the house and said, "I should really get back inside. Mama Dixon is fixing lunch, and I should be cleaning or starting the laundry or something."

Drew nodded, not wanting to push her and knowing she had a job to do. It was hard not to want to spend time with her, but he would see her at lunchtime.

"Alright, then," Drew said, holding tightly to Chance's rope. He wanted to give her a quick kiss but decided to wait and allow her to make the next move. After yesterday's conversation, he knew she needed to take things slow. He wouldn't be the one to rush things. He liked how things were going between the two of them, and he didn't want to mess them up. "See you at lunch?"

A red tint painted Becca's cheeks as she smiled back at him, confirming the answer to his question before turning away and heading back toward the house. He watched her leave, the sundress swaying in the breeze with every step she took. She caught him looking a time or two when she turned back to wave.

He let her go and turned his attention back to Chance. He wanted to invite her to supper tonight, just the two of them, but figured it could wait until later. He would work with the horse until Becca brought him lunch, and then he would make sure to ask her about having supper in the barn.

CHAPTER TWENTY

Becca couldn't believe Drew had asked her to supper in the barn over another shared lunch. She'd turned down his invitation the night before, but she didn't have the heart to turn him down again.

She'd finished up the list of things Mama Dixon had given her, and only when the last thing was crossed off the list, she asked to leave.

Allie still had her riding lessons, and while she was attending those, Becca planned to be home getting ready for her date night with Drew. He'd asked if she'd rather go somewhere in town, possibly check out Red's Bar and Grill, but she liked the idea of just the two of them without a lot of people around.

She stepped onto the porch and raised a hand over her eyes to block the sun as she focused on Drew and

Allie. Becca hadn't trusted Chance at first, but the long hours Drew had spent with him were paying off. The horse was coming around, and like Drew had said at lunch, before too long, he would introduce Chance to Simon and hopefully the two of them could go riding together.

She liked the idea, but she still wasn't too sure about climbing into a saddle. Maybe if Drew was with her... She was embarrassed to admit the unmentionable fear was still there, lurking in the shadows of her mind as she tried her best to overcome it.

"Allie," Becca called out as she neared the corral. Allie's attention turned from Drew as she focused on Becca. Becca waved her hand, motioning for Allie to come along with her. She'd thought about letting Allie stay a little while longer, knowing her mother would have no problem picking her up, but changed her mind and preferred to have her little girl home while she got ready for her night in with Drew.

"Can't I just stay here, Mama?" Allie tossed her head back and let out a defeated sigh when Becca explained why she couldn't. "Please?"

Becca wrapped an arm over her daughter's shoulders and guided her toward the car. It wasn't like Allie to throw a fit. "See you later," Becca called over her shoulder with a wave to Drew.

She slid into the driver's seat and started the car. She hadn't had the chance to talk to Allie about her and Drew. And since she'd be spending the evening with him, Becca decided it wouldn't hurt to let Allie know. They talked about the situation with her dad the night before, but Becca hadn't anticipated anything with Drew so soon, so that didn't factor into the conversation.

"I'm going to ask Nana to watch you for a little bit tonight, okay?" Becca asked, turning the car around in the driveway and pulling onto the highway. She would take her time driving home, allowing enough time to talk with Allie and make sure she was okay with Becca's budding relationship.

"What are we going to do?" Allie asked, crossing her arms over her chest and resting her head on the backseat. It was evident she was still upset about having to leave the Dixon Ranch so soon, but Becca wouldn't let her stay upset if she could help it.

"I'm sure you and Nana will find something to do," Becca said, smiling back at her daughter in the rearview mirror. "You two always seem to figure out a way to enjoy your time together."

Allie's eyes lit up as a smile pulled at her lips. "Maybe I'll ask her if we can make cotton candy with the carnival machine."

Becca smiled with a nod. "I'm sure she'd be okay with that."

Becca guided the car along the backroad, thinking of a way to start the conversation about her and Drew.

She wanted Allie to know about them dating, but she didn't want to get into all the details that would come along with it. Becca knew Allie still had questions about her father from their talk last night, and unfortunately, she couldn't answer for Chad. Only he could provide Allie with the answers to her questions, and since he was nowhere to be found, those questions would remain unanswered.

Becca prayed for Chad to come around, at least for Allie's sake. She wasn't too sure how she felt about sharing her little girl with the man who wrecked her life, but it wasn't about the two of them... it was about his relationship with his daughter.

There were so many thoughts going through her mind as she steered the car toward home. She glanced back at Allie who was now staring out the window from the backseat.

"Hey, baby," Becca said, pulling the car into the driveway and shifting into park before turning to face her daughter. Her plan to talk with Allie before getting home hadn't happened, but now that she was parked she would be able to give Allie her full attention. She knew her daughter had seen the two of them kiss, but she still wasn't sure how to ask Allie if she was okay with it. A part of her wanted to just move forward without talking to her daughter, but she knew deep down talking was the right thing to do. Even if Allie was quick to say she liked Drew and was okay with Becca spending more time with him, it would make Becca feel better.

"Why are we just sitting here? Shouldn't we go inside?" Allie asked with a furrowed brow. "I want to ask Nana about making cotton candy."

Becca smiled. "You'll have plenty of time to ask Nana while I'm getting ready."

Allie raised a brow, a look of confusion crossing her face, and Becca knew the question was coming before her little girl asked it. "Where are you going?"

Becca rested her hands in her lap and thought of the best way to say it. Would her daughter be okay with her spending more time with Drew? More than likely, yes. Would her daughter wonder why she was being left home while Becca had all the fun? Again, more than likely, yes.

"Drew invited me to supper tonight," Becca explained, waiting for Allie to express her concerns about that, but she was surprised when her daughter's eyes lit up and she cheered from the backseat. "You're okay with that? With me spending time with Drew?"

Allie nodded enthusiastically and said, "Uh huh. I like Drew. He's a lot nicer than my daddy was, but he also reminds me of daddy, too."

Relieved to know her daughter thought highly of Drew, Becca released a slow breath and waited to see where the conversation went from there. If Allie had questions, Becca would try her best to answer them.

"He always says that we need to make sure everything's okay with you before I do something," Allie said, rolling her eyes and letting out a sigh. "Just like Daddy used to."

Becca was relieved to know Drew respected her wishes even when she wasn't around to watch after Allie. It made her feel good to know that he took it seriously.

"Is Daddy ever coming back?"

The question hit Becca like a ton of bricks, and even though she had expected it last night during Allie's bathtime, she had been more than relieved when Allie hadn't asked then. Now, she found herself struggling to find the answer she'd come up with.

"Oh, baby, I don't know," Becca said, her tone soft and her voice just above a whisper. "He's... I'm not sure, baby. I'm sorry."

Allie wiped away the tears with the back of her hand, causing Becca's heart to break all over again. It didn't matter how prepared Becca had been while going through the divorce, seeing her daughter cry over her father was devastating.

"It's okay," Allie said, looking down at her hands as she played with her doll's dress. Becca's heart broke in a million pieces as she asked Allie to climb into the front seat. "Mama, don't cry. It's okay."

Becca reached out for her daughter and pulled her in close, wrapping her arms around her and holding her tightly against her chest. If there was one thing she prayed for, aside from everything being okay, it was for her daughter to find peace with her father's choice.

She kissed the top of her daughter's head and ran her hand through the blonde curls. "I know, baby," she said. "Everything's going to be okay. No matter what happens, you'll always have me and Nana who love you more than anything else in the world."

Allie nodded, snuggling herself into Becca's arms. "And Drew, too, Mama."

Becca smiled through the tears as she realized her daughter was right. Drew had more than proven that he cared about Allie, and that alone relieved most of Becca's worries. To know that a man could care about another man's child like his own was something Becca had only seen in the movies, and she thanked God that she'd found someone like Drew to look after Allie in a special way her own father couldn't.

"What do you say we head inside and ask Nana if she's okay with making some cotton candy?"

Allie jumped out of Becca's arms and scrambled out of the car as they headed inside. Becca would ask her mother to look after Allie for a couple of hours, promising it wouldn't be too late.

Before Becca had a chance to ask, though, Allie

beat her to it. "Nana, Mama's got a date tonight with Drew, and we get to make cotton candy," Allie called out as they walked in off the front porch. Becca kicked off her sandals and slid them out of the way of the door before following Allie through the living room and into the dining room.

"A date, huh?" her mother asked, a skeptical expression on her face. Becca nodded, letting her mother know it was true.

"I couldn't turn him down a second time," Becca admitted sheepishly, folding her hands in front of her as she took a seat at the table. "I was hoping that you'd be able to watch Allie tonight for a little bit since Drew asked me to supper."

Her mother's eyes lit up as she asked, "Is he taking you to Red's?"

Becca shook her head, knowing the evening would be a lot more special with just the two of them anyway. She didn't need the fancier things in life. She was happy with the basics. As long as her daughter was taken care of, that's all that mattered to her. Not some fancy meal at a restaurant.

"Well, okay, then," Becca's mother said, clapping her hands before standing from the kitchen table. "We better get things ready for a night of fun, Allie," she said as she booped Becca's daughter on the nose. "What do you say we go ahead and do that while your mom gets ready for her *date*?"

Allie nodded with a wide grin on her face as she stared at Becca. Becca winked and sent the girl into a fit of laughter. She just loved the relationship she shared with Allie and her mother.

"I won't be too late," Becca said.

"Take your time," her mother said with a knowing smile. If Becca hadn't known any better, she would have never guessed that her mother was referring to the conversation Becca had with Drew on his front porch. But she wouldn't put it past the two of them to eavesdrop on their conversation just to get a little bit more information about what was going on between them. Becca couldn't be mad with their attempt. They'd meant no harm in the way they'd gathered their information.

"You know I will," Becca said, offering her mother a quick wink before leaving the kitchen and heading for the bedroom. She needed to pick out something to wear and get ready before heading back to the Dixon Ranch.

CHAPTER TWENTY-ONE

Drew lit the candles and prayed Becca hadn't changed her mind. He'd given her an approximate time to meet him at the barn, and the minutes were slowly counting down.

He thought about the look on her face the first time he'd asked her to dinner with him. He should have known better than to put that kind of pressure on her, but from what he could tell, she was getting along better and better with everyone each day she worked.

Drew shrugged it off, realizing she would be there any minute. He made sure the plates were set just right, and the candles as well. He'd placed another bunch of wildflowers in a skinny vase he found floating around the house and set it on her side of the makeshift table.

The sun was setting off in the distance, tucking

itself behind the mountains as the sky provided a blanket of soft, warm pink and purple hues. It was the perfect night for dinner in the barn.

Drew glanced over his shoulder at the set-up. He'd never done anything like this before with anyone. If he were to be honest, he'd never put as much thought into another woman as he'd done for Becca.

Becca and Allie were the center of his attention now. His heart hadn't given him a choice in the matter. *It was a long time coming*, as his mother had said.

Drew had several thoughts running through his mind when he heard a familiar car pull up in the distance as the gravel crunched under the tires. He leaned against the old wood paneling and waited for Becca to make her way over to the barn.

She climbed out of the car, carefully shutting the door behind her. Drew watched as she made her way to the front of the car, hesitating a minute or two as she looked from the house to the barn. He'd never felt as nervous as he did tonight. His stomach was in all sorts of knots as he watched Becca make her way over to the barn.

"Hey, cowboy," she teased as she approached the barn. "I hear there's a dinner for two somewhere around here?"

He couldn't help but smirk at her failed attempt of

a drawl. Regardless of how horrible it had been, he gave her credit for being cute. Drew pushed away from the wooden exterior of the barn, wrapped his arm around her, and rested his hand on her lower back as he ushered her inside.

Drew heard her breath hitch at the sight in front of them. She looked from the makeshift table to him. "You did all this for me?"

Drew nodded, tipping his hat. "Sure did."

"And lasagna, too?" she asked as she made her way over to the food. She spun around to face him, and by the look on her face, Drew knew he'd done well. "Why do I have a feeling that our mothers had something to do with this?"

Drew half-laughed when he realized she was onto him. He might have asked them for a little bit of guidance while setting things up, but other than that, it had been all Drew.

"I recall hearing something about your mother burning lasagna one night," Drew said, kicking the dirt floor of the barn with the toe of his boot. "Mama Dixon and Carolyn must've done a lot of talking because before I knew it, Mama was whipping up a dinner for us, and low and behold... it's your favorite."

He motioned for Becca to sit down on a hay bale before taking a seat of his own across from her. He watched her take in everything in front of her. From the flowers to the food to the candles. She raised a brow and pointed at the candles in the middle of them. "Isn't it a bit dangerous to have candlelight dinners in a barn full of hay?"

Drew offered a subtle shrug and said, "I know a few good firemen."

Becca didn't like his answer all too well, but at least he saw a slight smile on her face as she smelled the flowers.

"These are beautiful," she said, glancing over at him. "You're getting better at not letting Simon get them first."

Drew shot a look over his shoulder at Simon, who was standing in the corner of his stall and minding his own business. Drew knew Simon would eat anything if given the chance.

He turned his attention back to Becca and smiled. He thought she was holding something back, not wanting to say whatever was on her mind. The conversation seemed stilted so far, and he couldn't help but feel as though he was waiting for the other shoe to drop.

"I've worked up a hefty appetite while putting all of this together," Drew said, shooting a wink and a grin at Becca. "What do you say we eat before it gets cold?"

Becca nodded and said grace before picking up her fork. Drew had never been one to say grace before a meal, but he liked that about Becca. He couldn't remember the last time he'd said grace, or even stepped foot inside church. Of course, he believed in God and all things holy, but he'd been on the road with the rodeo for so long...

"What are you thinking about?" Becca's question pulled him from his thoughts as he grabbed his fork and cut into the lasagna. He hesitated a minute, wondering what her reaction would be when he told her the truth.

"Just about how long it's been since I've been to church," he answered honestly, waiting for her to react, but she didn't.

Instead, she offered a kind smile and said, "I haven't been for a while now. I've been wanting to, but I just can't seem to find the courage to walk through the front door."

Drew took a bite of food and thought about what she'd said. He didn't think it'd take all that much to walk into church... His only problem was getting there in the first place.

"Courage?" he questioned, taking another bite as he tried piecing things together. "I'm not sure you'd need a lot of that to—"

Becca cut him off as she fidgeted with her napkin. He hadn't noticed how nervous she'd become in the last few minutes, and he couldn't help but wonder why.

"Things are just... different now," she said, hesitating a minute before she continued, "especially now that I have failed at marriage."

Drew heard her loud and clear. He wasn't quite sure what to say to make her feel better about her situation, but he wanted her to know there was no judgment as far as he could see. Marriage wasn't for the weak, and he knew it took a lot of patience, along with loyalty and trust, to make it work. He'd thought a few times about what he'd do if he found the right woman to settle down with, but he'd shrugged it off... or at least until he'd met Becca and Allie.

"I should go," Becca said, setting her fork down beside her plate and preparing to leave. Drew could see the torment in her eyes as she looked up at him. He wanted to take it all away from her, tell her it would be okay. Whatever she was facing from the past would eventually go away. But he wasn't sure what her past entailed other than a cheating ex who was also Allie's father.

"Look," Drew said, trying his best to understand. "I'm not too sure about everything that's happened, but I do know that I'm not here to judge you."

Becca nodded as she took a drink of wine. He could tell she didn't want to talk much about it, but he just needed her to know that everyone had a past to deal with—she wasn't alone. The only thing that mattered was surviving and making it out stronger in the end.

"I'm…"

Her words trailed off, and Drew's stomach filled with knots. He wanted nothing more than for them to enjoy a nice dinner together, just the two of them. He'd put everything in place just right, and now he had a feeling it was about to fall apart.

He had patience, but her struggle to tell him what was on her mind was testing him. He hated to see her upset. Whatever it was that she was holding back, Drew had to find a way of getting her to understand it wouldn't change the way he felt about her.

"Drew, I'm just not sure about anything right now."

He heard her loud and clear. The words she was refusing to say were even louder than the words she'd already said. She was having second thoughts about everything, but mainly it had to be about *this*. *Them*.

"Bec, this was just supposed to be a nice dinner," he said, setting his drink down before reaching for her hand. "Just the two of us without a worry in the world to think about."

Becca slowly nodded. When her eyes met his, Drew could see the tears. She was definitely having second thoughts, and he wasn't so sure he knew what to say to make her change her mind.

"I'm sorry," she said, grabbing a napkin and

drying her eyes. He wanted to take away her pain. He wanted to make her realize that whatever happened in the past wasn't going to happen again.

"Don't be sorry," Drew said, standing now and pulling her to her feet in front of him. He wrapped his arm around her and pulled her close. "Bec, I care about you more than anything else. I know you've been through a lot in the last few months, and I'm sorry that you have, but that doesn't change how I feel about you."

When she didn't say anything, he continued, "You and Allie have a special place in my heart, and I'm going to do whatever I can to show you how much you two mean to me."

Becca inhaled a deep breath and released it slowly as she relaxed against his chest. He tightened his hold and kissed the top of her head. He could only imagine the thoughts running through her mind, questioning everything he was telling her and wondering if he was just like the one she'd left behind. He didn't know who the guy was that had done her wrong, and it didn't matter anyway. He would never be like that—no matter what other people might say about him.

"But what about the rodeo?"

Her words were soft spoken, but they held an edge. He could hear the doubt in her voice as he thought about the answer to her question. The rodeo had meant a lot to him, there was no doubt about that, but more than Becca and Allie combined? Not a chance.

"What about it?" he asked, wanting her to say whatever was on her mind. He didn't like how she held back. He wanted her to feel comfortable with talking to him about things—especially if it had anything to do with them.

She gently shrugged her shoulders and took a step back, her eyes looking everywhere but on him. He gently placed a finger underneath her chin and lifted it slightly so she would have no choice but to look at him.

"You've gotta talk to me, Becca," he pleaded, searching her eyes for any sign of what she was thinking. There was no telling what kind of thoughts were traveling through her mind, but he could only imagine they weren't too pleasant. "I don't know what you're thinking if you don't tell me. I don't know what to say if you can't tell me what's bothering you."

Judging by the concerned look on her face, she was having doubts about them. She'd mentioned the rodeo, and Drew had a feeling she didn't like the thought of him returning to the circuit once his injury healed.

She let out a long sigh and said, "I'm not sure where to start."

Drew offered a slight grin. Trying to ease her into

conversation, he said, "Start wherever you'd like. We've got all night."

Becca let out a soft laugh and shook her head. "No, we really don't. I promised Allie I'd be back in time to tuck her into bed."

"Okay, then you better start talking because time's a tickin'," he said with a playful grin, and Becca laughed. "I'm interested in knowing what you've got to say about the rodeo."

Becca looked over her shoulder and back at him. He patiently waited for her to say something, but when she didn't, he asked, "You think I'm going to run off as soon as this arm of mine is healed and leave the two of you behind?"

She answered his question with a slight nod. He'd had a feeling that was what had been weighing on her mind all this time, but he hadn't felt like bringing it up until she'd mentioned it first.

"I'm not sure what I'm going to do about all that," he said, knowing that answer wasn't the one she was hoping to hear. He couldn't tell her that he wasn't going back to chasing rodeos and riding bulls. "Look, Bec, for what it's worth, I like you... a lot. And I'm not sure what you're needing from me right now, but I don't want to ruin whatever it is we have going on. I know you've got a lot of things going on, and I know you're worried about everything. I get it."

He looked down at Becca and waited for her to

say something, but instead she nodded and leaned into him. He secured his arm around her and kissed the top of her head. He wasn't a man of many words, especially in a moment like this, but he was trying. It was hard to stand there in front of Becca while knowing she was having doubts about them. Knowing that she was seconds away from calling an end to what they'd shared, all because of the fear and torment from her past. He didn't want to lose Becca, or Allie. He wanted them in his life.

CHAPTER TWENTY-TWO

Becca's heart raced as thoughts filled her mind. She wanted nothing more than to believe Drew when he told her everything would be okay and that she had nothing to worry about.

She'd always been one to trust her instincts, and right now, they were telling her to believe Drew. To lean on him and allow him to get close. But no matter how much she wanted to, tried to, she just couldn't shake the feeling that something horrible was going to happen.

She breathed in deeply, inhaling his scent as he held her close to him. Becca had arrived at the ranch with good intentions and high hopes. She'd planned for a nice evening spent with Drew without being interrupted by negative thoughts. But all of that seemed to crumble around her as the weight of the unknown crept over her and settled in.

No matter how many conversations she'd had with her mother, and no matter how much Drew swore he cared about Becca and Allie… it wasn't enough. *Would it ever be enough?*

Becca didn't know the answer as she looked up at Drew. His eyes filled with worry and disheartening expectancy. She hated to be the one to tell him that she wasn't right for him. Her heart felt too betrayed to ever love again, and none of that was Drew's fault.

"I should get going," she said with a breathless whisper. She fought back the rush of emotions as she stared into his eyes, knowing he was not only hearing her silent rejection, but feeling it too. "It's getting late, and I'm sure Allie is waiting for me."

She shifted her weight as she took a step back, careful to take it slow so she wouldn't have another mishap in the barn. She willed herself to hold it together as she turned and walked away. Becca prayed Drew would let her leave without a fight because she was only doing what she felt was best for everyone involved—including Drew.

She made it as far as she could before Drew called out to her, causing her heart to still as she stood frozen near the door.

"Becca."

She'd never felt so conflicted in her entire life.

Until now, she'd only ever loved her husband—*ex-husband*. And now, because of Chad, she was left picking up the pieces and mending her broken heart while praying she'd make it through and learn to love again… to trust again.

"If it's because…"

His words trailed off, causing her to hesitate a minute as she expected him to say something further. "Drew, it's not—"

He tipped his head back and let out an exasperated sigh. "I get it. It's the whole *it's not you, it's me* deal," he said, his tone falling flat with a subtle hint of annoyance. "I'm not sure what else I can say, or *do*, to prove how much I care about you, Bec. I care about you *and* Allie. You said you needed time. That's okay," he assured her, close enough once again to trace her jawline with his thumb. "I'm giving you all the time you need."

She really should have made a run for her car when she'd had the chance. She didn't want to cry anymore. She didn't want to be the woman who resented her ex for falling in love with another woman. She certainly didn't want to be the woman who now had trust issues and couldn't find it in her heart to love again, no matter how amazing the man standing in front of her appeared to be. But there she was, standing in front of Drew and expressing her rollercoaster of emotions and fears while trying her best to remain the strong woman she knew she'd been all along.

"I'm sorry, Drew," she said, taking one final step away from him as she silently pleaded that he'd let her leave this time. She couldn't spend another minute in front of him while the push and pull of emotions and bewildering thoughts ambushed her. She felt foolish for leading him on, for making him believe she was able to have a relationship, just to take it all away and cause everything to crash down around her once again.

"I'll be here when you're ready" were the last words she heard before climbing into her car and heading home for the night.

Pulling into her mother's driveway, Becca ran a hand through her hair and checked her reflection. She knew it would be obvious to her mother the minute she walked in the door that the evening spent with Drew hadn't gone as planned, and Becca felt comforted in knowing her mother would understand.

Becca grabbed her purse from the passenger seat and stepped out of her car, catching a glimpse of the truck parked in the street. Her heart plummeted to her stomach at the realization of who owned the vehicle. If she had thought for one minute her night could not have gotten worse, she'd been proven wrong by an all-too-familiar Chevy Silverado.

"Chad," she whispered under her breath as she

hurried up the porch steps and pushed through the front door. "Allie," Becca called out, dropping her purse at the door and making her way to the room filled with soft conversation. "Mama," Becca said, rounding the corner of the living room and coming face to face with the man who turned not only her world upside down, but her daughter's as well.

Becca's eyes looked from Allie, who was sitting happily nestled against Chad's chest, to her mother. Her mother offered her a subtle shrug along with a half-hearted smile, telling Becca the one thing she already knew—his visit had been unannounced and completely unexpected.

"Bec," Chad said, giving Allie a quick pat to get her to let him off the couch. Becca shook her head as he made his way over to her. She braced herself against the doorjamb and prayed for God to give her the strength she needed.

"Don't," she said, raising her hand in front of her and stopping him before he had a chance to get closer. Thankfully, he stopped short after realizing Becca had no intention to share pleasantries. "What are you doing here?" she asked quietly, her words sharp.

Chad glanced over his shoulder, looking back at Becca's little girl—*their* little girl—and said, "I just wanted to stop in and see how my girls are doing."

Becca cringed and took a step back, her arms

remaining crossed in front of her. Everything about his visit had her guard up as she focused on him.

"Why don't we go on into your room and color a picture for your father?" Becca's mother asked Allie, leading her from the living room and down the hallway toward her bedroom. Becca silently thanked her mother, knowing the conversation between her and Chad would be easier without worrying whether or not Allie would hear it.

Chad smiled and waved at Allie, telling her he'd be right there and couldn't wait to see the picture. He turned to Becca, taking her in from head to toe—something she had once enjoyed before he'd decided to step out.

"What are you doing here?" she asked again, refusing to let it go until she got the answer she was looking for. There was no good coming out of his visit tonight, and no matter how happy Allie appeared to be, Becca knew her daughter would be left crying when her father decided to walk out the door once more.

"I, uh," Chad stammered, taking a look around the house and gathering what Becca could only imagine to be the little bit of concern he truly had for Becca and Allie. He ran a hand through his hair. Unlike Drew's, Chad kept his hair long and matted. He looked rough, with bags under his eyes and more than a five o'clock shadow along with the stubble of his chin. If Becca hadn't known any better, she'd guess it was from lack of sleep and working late hours. But she knew now what she hadn't known then... he'd spent late nights with a woman other than her, and he drowned what little conscience he had with alcohol. Apparently, from his disheveled appearance, that's exactly what he'd been doing right before arriving at her mother's house. "I miss you, Bec."

She shook her head and wedged a hand between them, forcing him to keep his distance. There was no reason to allow him any closer. She wanted nothing to do with him, and she prayed that he would walk right out the door and leave for good.

"Tell me that you haven't missed me," he said, stepping closer and closing the distance between them, the smell of alcohol strong on his breath as she shied away from him. It hurt too much to look him the eye after everything he'd done. And for him to stand there now, in front of her, and to pretend nothing happened and everything was back to normal with them? He had another thing coming.

"I haven't," she said matter-of-factly without missing a beat. She didn't need to hear his sob story excuse of an apology or whatever else he'd come there to say. "We've been doing fine on our own."

He took a step back, as though her words had smacked him across the face. "I've missed my girls."

She never felt so much anger for another person

until now. She was trying her best to let it go and to move on, but now that he was standing in front of her, she wouldn't back down. She wouldn't have a change of heart.

"I want you to come back home, Bec. You and Allie need to come home with me," he pleaded with a furrowed brow. "We need to put our family back together and make things work."

Becca shook her head, checking the clock on the wall. She'd cut her evening short with Drew to be able to home for Allie, but she had a sudden realization that maybe her instincts had been trying to warn her about what was waiting for her at home. As if they knew Chad was up to no good and it would take more than Becca's mother and Allie to make him leave.

But right now, standing in front of Chad, listening to him go on about how much he loved Becca and how much they needed to be a family again, Becca knew he wasn't leaving anytime soon.

She thought about her purse near the door, where she could possibly grab it and call the Dixons without Chad knowing…

Becca hesitated, wondering if maybe she was overreacting. She'd just left the ranch, and the look on Drew's face when she'd pulled out of the driveway…

"You need to leave, Chad," she said, pointing toward the door. She wasn't sure where the night was headed, but she didn't want him there. She knew it would break Allie's heart to see Chad leave yet again, but he was no good for them. Her mind flashed back to the same thought she'd had at one time about Drew.

"But wait, Bec," Chad said, stumbling toward her and righting himself as he leaned against the wall. "Please give me another chance to make things better with us. I miss you. I mean it."

Becca held strong, keeping her emotions under control as she refused to budge. "I'm sure you do, but it's no longer about us," Becca said, releasing a heavy sigh when she caught Allie watching from the hallway with her Nana standing behind her, trying to convince her to go back to her room. Allie refused to go anywhere, and Becca knew exactly what her daughter was thinking—she'd never see her father again if she left the hallway. Tears clouded Becca's vision as she tried to focus on Chad and his insincere advances. She couldn't care less about what he promised her. All of that went in one ear and out the other. She only cared about one thing—Allie.

"Daddy, please don't go," Allie whispered through tears as Becca's mother held onto her shoulders. "I miss you."

Becca looked from Allie to her mother and back to Chad, who was now figuring out his next move. Becca didn't want to stop him from seeing Allie. That wasn't what she wanted to do at all. He'd made the decision to leave the two of them without anywhere to go when he'd called it quits on their marriage.

With a loud grunt, Chad turned toward the door and said something under his breath Becca couldn't quite understand as he walked onto the front porch. Allie raced after him, stopping him on his way down the porch steps.

"Why can't you stay?"

Becca stepped onto the front porch and wrapped a comforting arm around her daughter as Allie searched her father's eyes for the answers to her questions. Becca couldn't shield her daughter from the hurt she was about to experience. Her father might have been standing there in front of them, but Becca wasn't sold on the thought of Chad wanting them back in his life.

Without a word, Chad ignored Allie and climbed into his truck. Becca held onto her daughter, knowing the wave of emotion was coming and knowing the damage Chad had created tonight.

Becca watched as Chad pulled away from the curb in front of her mother's house, leaving the two of them behind once again. It had been hard to keep her emotions in check while Chad had been standing in front of her, but it was even harder now to do just the same as Allie leaned into her and sobbed, gripping tightly to the picture she'd colored for her father.

CHAPTER TWENTY-THREE

It had been a couple of days since Drew had seen Becca or Allie. His mother hadn't heard anything either, and that alone caused him to worry that Becca might have not only walked away from him, but quit her job at the ranch as well. A part of him worried she might even leave town.

"I'm heading into town," Drew called out to his brothers who were herding the cattle from one pasture to the next in an attempt to keep the pastures from being overgrazed. Soon, they would be hauling a few to Clayton Mitchell, the owner of the meat locker and deli in Maple Glen—a connection they'd made thanks to their uncle Curt. They would gladly sell their cattle as needed if that meant it'd keep the ranch running.

He climbed into the driver's seat in the cab of his truck and turned the key. The old truck roared to life, but it still wasn't loud enough to sound out the worried thoughts racing through his mind.

If Becca wasn't ready for a relationship, he wouldn't push it. He was more than willing to give her the space and time she needed. But right now, his only thought was to make sure she was okay. It wasn't like Allie to miss riding lessons, and it wasn't like Becca to not let his mother know she'd be gone from work.

He couldn't stop thinking about the what ifs and wondering if maybe Becca knew something he didn't. She'd been holding back and not telling him everything for a while now, which had been completely okay with him, until it wasn't... and it now caused Drew to wonder what had happened since she'd left.

He guided his truck along the road, steering it around the sharp curves and bends in the highway leading him into town. He thought about what might have happened if somehow her ex showed up at her mother's house. Or what might have happened the night after she'd left the barn.

There was too much going through his mind as he closed the distance between him and Carolyn Adams' house. He rounded the corner, pressing on the brakes as he pulled up in front of the house. Becca's car was parked in the drive, and Allie was playing with a friend on the front porch.

Drew grabbed his cowboy hat from the passenger

seat and slid it on as he climbed out of his truck. He was surprised to find that nothing much had changed in the last few days. As far as he could tell, everything was still how Becca had described living with her mother.

He made his way to the front porch, catching Allie's attention as his boot caught the first step. Her eyes locked on his, and her face lit up with a wide smile. She quickly scrambled to her feet and raced over to him, wrapping her arms around him in an excited bear hug.

He checked for any sign of Becca but didn't see her.

"I've missed you," Allie said, her blonde curls bouncing as she pulled away from him and jumped up and down. "Mama said we needed to take a break for a while. That I could only play with Rosie and that's it."

Drew looked down at the girl who must have been Rosie and smiled at the young girl who had to be the same age as Allie, if not a year or two younger. "Well, I've missed you too," he said, climbing one porch step at a time. "Is your mother inside?"

Allie nodded and said, "Her and Nana are drinking coffee and probably still talking about my dad."

Drew hesitated before knocking on the door. He

couldn't make heads or tails out of what Allie meant, but he was certain to find out eventually.

He rapped his knuckles against the wooden frame of the screen door and patiently waited for either Carolyn or Becca to answer as he listened to the young girls play with their dolls on the porch floor behind him.

"Well, Drew," Carolyn announced more than greeted while plastering a half-smile on her face. If he knew any better, he could see a slight sense of relief cross her face as she invited him into her house.

Drew reached up and removed his hat from his head and held it firmly in front of him. His heart raced with a mixture of adrenaline and uncertainty as he looked around the front room in search of the main reason he'd stopped by.

"Becca's in the kitchen," Carolyn stated. Then she leaned in and whispered, "She's had a rough couple of days since Chad's last visit, but I think she'll be okay."

As he toed off his boots, Carolyn added, "I think she'll be happy to see you."

He wasn't too sure about any of that. He had a feeling the last person Becca cared to see would be him, otherwise she would have made it a point to come out to the ranch.

He followed Carolyn's lead into the kitchen where

she soon left the two of them alone and ushered herself out the same way they'd walked in.

"Hey," he greeted softly, walking around to the other side of the table and standing in front of Becca. Becca was the most beautiful woman he'd ever met in his life, but right now, she looked rough. Tears stained her cheeks, and the makeup she'd been wearing was no longer held in place, but instead, streaked down her face in the path of fallen tears. "Becca, what's going on? Is everything alright?"

She dabbed at her eyes, attempting to pull herself together as she shook her head. He reached out to her, and she pulled away. He realized he might not have been ready for any of this after all, but he wouldn't regret coming to see her. Something told him that she needed him now more than ever. Not because she was dependent on him and unworthy to hold her own, but for comfort and understanding she wasn't used to receiving from her past.

"I can't do this anymore," Becca whispered through hushed tears. "It's too much. I can't keep her away from him, and maybe I was wrong for leavi—"

"Whoa," he said, holding a hand out and motioning for her to slow down. "What's this all about?" he asked gently before correcting himself. "I mean, I have a good feeling I already know, but what's all this about being wrong and not keeping Allie from him?"

Becca let out a long breath and explained everything to him, letting everything out that she'd been holding back for so long. It took everything he had to fight the urge to reach out and touch her, hold her... but she'd made it clear that she didn't want that—at least not right now.

"He seemed so..."

Her words trailed off, and Drew thought of a few he could help her out with, but none that would have been charitable. He couldn't imagine letting his love for a woman like Becca slip through the cracks. No matter how heavily temptation weighed, it would never weigh enough to shove her aside. And not to mention Allie...

"Becca," he whispered softly, hesitating before reaching out once more and placing his hand on top of hers, thankful she didn't pull away this time. "I'm sorry. I can't imagine what all of this has to be like for you. For Allie. I can't imagine what kind of man... if he's even a man at all," he paused and said, "could do what he has done."

Becca dried the tears with a quick dab of her napkin and nodded.

"I know I'm the last person you want to see right now, and I—"

Becca shook her head, interrupting him mid-sentence. "That's not true at all. I'm just in a really bad place right now, and I'm not sure what I'm supposed to do. I have so much on my mind," she said, running a hand through the waves in her hair as Drew listened intently. He waited for her to tell him what she needed from him. What she wanted, or needed, him to do next. He didn't want to just sit back and wait for whatever to happen. He wanted to be right there with her, alongside her to make sure she knew that she could count on him for anything.

He wasn't being pushy, because his mother had raised him better than that, but he wasn't going to back down and walk away. Taking challenges head on was a part of him, and this was one challenge he refused to give in to.

"I'm sorry I'm such a mess," Becca said in an outward cry. "I'm sorry for leading you to believe I was ready for something more when clearly I'm not."

Drew offered her hand a gentle, reassuring squeeze as he looked into her eyes. "Becca, I don't care how big of a mess you think you are, I beg to differ," he said with a slight grin. "You're a strong, determined woman who is a wonderful mother and, not to mention, the fact that you're beautiful and everything I've ever wanted to find in a woman."

He meant every word he'd said, but he'd put a spin on it in order to make Becca smile. It had worked as planned when he saw a smile pull at her lips and her eyes focus on his.

"I know that you need time," he said, remembering how he'd overstepped when he arrived at the house in the first place and feeling the need to justify his reasoning for being there. "I'm not here to push you into a relationship with me. I'm here to show you that I care. I don't care if we're forever friends and nothing more than that," he promised, "I'll still be right here waiting for you. You have my word, Bec."

She silently wiped away the fresh tears streaming down her face as he pulled her up from the spot she'd been sitting and wrapped his arm around her. He pulled her close and kissed her forehead, feeling the connection he'd missed the last few days. He couldn't explain the feeling Becca had stirred inside of him. Something that had changed his mind about a few things—one of them being settling down and raising a family of his own. He'd been just as shocked the day he'd thought about it, not wanting to tell anyone for fear they'd call his bluff and he wouldn't have anything to show for it. But now, standing in Carolyn Adams' kitchen with Becca in front of him, there was no doubt he had what he wanted, and he wouldn't let it go without a fight.

"As long as you promise me that you'll still be here tomorrow, and that you're okay, I'm going to head back home," Drew said, tipping her chin and looking her in the eyes. She nodded, giving him the answer he'd hoped for while holding her. "I'm not going anywhere. I'm right here for you, and for Allie. No matter what."

She nodded, burrowing her face into his chest as he held her close to him. He didn't want to leave her, but he respected her enough to give her the space and time she'd need to clear her mind and figure things out.

He gave her one last kiss, relieved when she didn't pull away, before grabbing his hat from the back of the chair and heading out of the house. He'd say one last goodbye to Allie, and he'd head back home to the ranch to help his brothers while Becca took the time she needed.

"See ya later, Allie-gator," he called out with a smile on his face as he walked onto the front porch. Allie's eyes widened in surprise as she caught onto what he'd learned from her and Carolyn.

"Afterwhile, Crocodile," she sang out, along with her friend.

"Gotta go, Buffalo," he said with a laugh as he approached his truck and opened the door.

"See you soon, Raccoon," Allie called out with a smile on her face as she waved goodbye.

Drew climbed into the front seat of his truck and started the engine. He could only pray he'd see them again soon. It was all up to the good Lord and Becca.

CHAPTER TWENTY-FOUR

Becca had called Mama Dixon to let her know she wasn't planning to return to the ranch for at least a few days. She voluntarily included the reason for her absence, which heavily weighed on Chad's return. Becca wanted to make sure to be home if he decided to stop by the house again. She hated to think he would do something foolish, like take Allie from her, and she prayed to God that he never would, but after seeing him, it felt safer to distance herself and give them plenty of time at home together.

Becca tried to make it fun for Allie, but her little girl wasn't having it. She'd tried to play tic-tac-toe, Connect Four, and other board games they had laying around the house, but Allie still shook her head as she twirled her hair around her tiny fingers.

"I miss them," Allie said, giving her mother a pleading look that silently begged her to change her mind about the Dixon Ranch, but more importantly, Drew.

Becca found a comfortable spot on the couch next to Allie and hooked her arm around her shoulders in a side hug.

"I know, baby," Becca said, "and I'm sorry. It's for the best right now, okay?"

Allie pushed away and scooted down from Becca. Becca hated seeing her daughter so upset, especially when she felt she was doing the right thing. Parenting was hard as it was without having to explain every decision in the nicest way possible. Sometimes, no matter how much Becca would have loved her decisions to come easily, some just didn't.

"Don't you miss him, too, Mama?" Allie's eyes filled with tears as her bottom lip quivered. Becca had spent the last two nights talking to Allie about additional information that had happened between her and Chad, excluding the details that were not kid friendly, and then spent another hour talking about her and Drew. She'd mentioned high hopes a time or two, and the possibility of things seeming almost too good to be true. No matter how honest she was about everything, her daughter still refused to believe that Becca could decide to walk away from the ranch, and Drew, like that. It was hard for her six-year-old daughter to wrap her head around the reality of adult relationships and the problems associated with heartbreak, but Becca would continue to try her best to make Allie understand.

"Yes, I miss him, baby," she said, feeling her heart ache at the thought of watching him leave. She recalled how his gentle teasing back and forth with Allie had stirred something inside of her as she watched out the front window. He'd been so calm after she'd asked him to leave. He respected her enough to leave without being asked twice, and because of that, Becca knew he was a good man. But that didn't mean he was good enough for her and Allie… She couldn't trust that he wouldn't leave her like Chad had done…

"I miss him *and* Simon, Mama." Her daughter pouted. "And Chance, too."

Her daughter jutted out her bottom lip, and Becca shook her head with a soft exhale of air. "I haven't even gotten to truly meet Chance all that much, and now I'm never going to."

Allie's dramatic outcries were too much. If she hadn't thought about putting her daughter through acting lessons, there was no better time than now. Her theatrics were certainly on point.

"And what about my riding lessons, Mama?" Allie pleaded, "Are those going to stop, too?"

Becca leaned her head back against the couch and

stared at the ceiling. How was she going to break it to her daughter that she didn't think they could continue on the Dixon ranch? Why was parenting so hard? Why was adulting even harder?

"Allie," Becca's mother called from the dining room. "Why don't you go on and take a bath while your mama and I have a talk, okay?"

Without argument, Allie stood from the couch. "I get to color with my new bath markers," she announced, racing down the hallway.

Soon, Becca heard the bathroom door creak shut, and she called out for Allie to leave it cracked open just in case she needed their help. A few seconds later, the door slid open just enough to allow a sliver of light to shine into the hallway.

"Thank you," Becca called down the hallway.

She heard the splashing of water and a quick, "You're welcome, Mama."

Becca's mother patted Becca on the arm and offered a tender smile. "I'll be with her in a minute," she said. "I just wanted to see how you're holding up."

Her mother had witnessed everything from Chad's unwelcomed arrival to her basically pushing Drew out the front door, pleading everyone to give her time and space to get things figured out. Without judgment, her mother continued to be there for her—at the ready for much-needed advice.

"I'm fine," Becca lied. She was everything but fine, and her mother would know it.

"I've seen you *fine* before, and it looked nothing like this *fine*," her mother said, giving Becca a playful once-over. Becca shrugged. She wasn't sure what her mother expected her to say. She hadn't had the time to process everything with Chad before walking out the door and filing for a divorce. And now that she was back home, in a whole different world than what she'd left behind, she needed time to figure things out.

"I'm just…"

Her words trailed off, and her mother finished her sentence without a second thought. "Scared? Alone? Feeling uncertain?"

Becca shook her head and frowned. "I know you know, Ma," Becca said, tucking a stray hair behind her ear. The same stray hair Drew had been the one to tuck numerous times during their close encounters. "It's just…"

"I get it," her mother said, patting Becca's arm. "You're doing the best you can with what you've been dealt, and from the looks of it, the first few cards weren't fair."

Becca cracked up at her mother's analogy but knew her mother had a point. The hand Becca had been dealt in her marriage had looked like a royal flush, but instead had flopped. Now, she was staring at the possibility of another royal flush, something that didn't come all too often and was more or less unheard of happening twice in the same game.

"But, thankfully, you're able to turn those cards in and ask for a better hand," her mother stated. "And I know deep down you'll play the cards the way you feel is right, but I just hope that you know Drew's something special. I've seen the way he looks at you, and looks after Allie."

Deep down, Becca knew it, too. But she couldn't shake the pressing notion that hearts would break regardless of what she chose, and it was only a matter of time before Drew was the one who broke her already broken heart.

"But it's only a matter of time..." Becca said, allowing her words to trail off and knowing her mother already knew they were coming by the look on her face.

"Becca," her mother said, "I think hearts are already broken. It's time to mend them together and give love, and *Drew*, a chance."

Becca's mother patted her on the leg and offered a gentle, reassuring squeeze before standing up from the couch. She hooked a thumb over her shoulder and said, "I'm going to head in there to finish up her bath, but I want you to think about what I've said, okay?"

Becca nodded as her mother turned to leave the living room and was surprised when she spun around and said, "For what it's worth, I like Drew, and I think he'll make an excellent son-in-law someday."

"Get out of here," she said, grabbing the square pillow beside her and flinging it at her mother.

When her mother was out of the room and down the hallway, Becca leaned back and thought about what she had said. Things wouldn't always come easily, Becca knew that much to be true. But things didn't always have to be difficult either, and that was something Becca was still learning.

CHAPTER TWENTY-FIVE

Drew was all about giving Becca the time she needed, but he wouldn't deny how crazy it was making him without knowing what to expect. He'd left the ball in Becca's court when he left her house, and it killed him to know she might decide not to be with him. She'd given him a small glimpse of hope of settling down and actually having something worth sticking around home for...

"What are you moping around about?" Blake asked, walking up the steps behind him. Drew spun to face his brother and furrowed a brow. "I'm not moping."

Blake shot his head back and let out a fake laugh. "You could've fooled me," he said, patting Drew on the back with a firm hand. "You've got no one to blame but yourself."

Drew stopped mid-stride and dropped the hand he had resting on the door handle before looking back at Blake. He'd heard a lot of fighting words come out of his siblings' mouths, but nothing had ever affected him quite like this.

"How are you figuring it's my fault?" Drew asked, jamming a finger into his chest.

Blake took a step back and raised his hands in front of him. "Easy, Cujo," he said, tossing their other brother a crooked smile and looking back at Drew. Garrett stood off to the side now, preparing for Drew to take a swing. Maybe if they'd been ten years younger, he might've thought about rolling in the dirt a few times. But he was getting too old for any of that now. He worked too hard and was already sore after a hard day's work.

"She's just needing some time is all," Drew assured his brothers, looking between the two of them for argument. "I'm just giving her the space she needs."

Garrett tossed his head back this time, catching a glare from both Drew and Blake. "What? We've all heard that a time or two, haven't we? Almost every girl in high school told me that more than once or twice."

"Do you blame them?" Drew asked, dodging his brother's quick response of a slug and laughing harder. "I mean, come on…"

"What do you know about love, anyway?" Garrett asked, glaring over at Drew without discriminating against Blake.

Blake stepped back and raised his hands up. "I didn't say anything about nothing," he said, and Drew laughed.

"Come on, Gare Bear," Drew said, taking his brother in a one-armed headlock. "What do you know about love?"

Garrett tapped out and gave Drew a slight shove. "More than you, obviously."

Drew wouldn't put it past either of his brothers to know more about the *L* word. It wasn't like Drew to get caught up in feelings and all those crazy things related to falling hard for someone. He'd spent more time chasing eight seconds than he'd ever spent chasing after a girl. Most girls never liked him enough to give him a shot anyway, so it was a moot point to argue with Garrett. The rodeo was his entire existence. Or at least, it had been until recently, and whether or not Becca had anything to do with that was yet to be determined.

"What about what's her name?" Drew asked, drawing the attention back to Garrett just to give him a little bit of a hard time. Take the heat off his back for a little bit.

"Shyann," Garrett answered without missing a beat.

"Whoa, you had her name at the ready," Drew said, drawing fake pistols from the side of his legs and pretending to shoot targets. "Pew pew."

Garrett shook his head, a failed attempt to hide the laugh he was holding back. Drew nodded, affirming what he already knew about his brother and Shyann. They'd been an item for a while until she decided to up and leave Woodford Creek and head for the city. Something about not wanting to follow in her mother's footsteps and marry a rancher. Drew remembered how upset Garrett had been, and he honestly couldn't blame the guy. Shyann had grown up across the creek from the Dixons and had been through thick and thin with them. Every time there was ever a problem on the ranch, Shyann was the first to help out. It was too bad when she decided the small-town life on a ranch was no longer the life she wanted to live.

"I wonder what's going to happen with that place now that Ol' Man Riggs isn't around to take care of it anymore," Drew said, glancing off in the distance toward the creek dividing the two properties. He'd heard the news about the old man's passing shortly after he'd arrived in town. "From the look of the place, it'll be a hard sell."

Garrett stared off in the distance, and Drew wondered what was going through his brother's mind. He hadn't meant to stir up old, buried feelings. That hadn't been his intention. It was just a passing thought that slipped out before he could think twice.

"Yeah, that place needs a lot of work," Garrett mumbled before turning back toward the house. He made his way over to the wooden rocking chair and sat down. "I hate to think that Ol' Man Riggs had let it get that bad."

"I think I've seen someone over there checking on the livestock," Blake said, shading his eyes as he looked off toward the property. Drew had heard the property was in dire need of help, but it hadn't been like Mr. Riggs to ask for it. "But who knows?"

Drew shrugged when Garrett didn't say anything about the Riggs's farm. He'd thought about lending a hand or two throughout the years, but after Garrett and Shyann had a falling out, Drew thought it was best to stay on their own side of the creek for a while.

"So what are your plans with the new horse?" Blake asked, hooking a thumb over his shoulder and looking right at Drew.

Drew took a look at the black horse running along the fence in the pasture and said, "Well, Chance is coming along quite well, actually. It won't be too much longer before he's ready to be saddled up."

"Chance, huh?" Blake asked, staring back at him. "That's not a name I'd expect for you to give a horse."

His brothers shot him a knowing grin, and Drew

was proud of himself for letting a six-year-old name the horse. "Allie named him. I kinda like it," he said. "It's even better now because of her reason behind giving him that name."

Garrett and Blake exchanged glances right before Garrett called him out. "When did you become such a softy?"

Drew laughed and offered a quick shrug. "It happens to the best of us, I guess."

Blake slugged him in the good arm and said, "Don't worry. It looks good on you."

Garrett placed his head in his hands and said, "Wow. One minute he's a big, bad rodeo star, and the next he's naming horses Chance with a kid that ain't even his."

Blake caught Drew before he had a chance to knock Garrett's hat off. "Let it go," Blake demanded, tossing a glare over his shoulder at Garrett who played dumb. "I didn't mean anything by it. Calm down."

Drew didn't care whether or not he meant it, he took it the way he'd said it. "It doesn't matter if Allie's mine or not. Since when do we pick and choose who we love and care about?"

Blake released his shirt from his grip and took a step back. He held his hands up between them and asked, "You two good?"

Drew nodded, amazed that he'd actually thrown

the *L* word out when referencing Allie, and if he were to be honest, it applied to Becca, too.

"Just keep your thoughts to yourself," Drew warned Garrett before heading into the house. He'd had enough of his brothers for the night. He needed to get in and wash up before suppertime.

"How's everything going out there?"

His mother greeted him near the door, and for a minute, Drew thought about turning around and heading right back outside. He didn't want to have a heart-to-heart conversation about Becca and Allie with his mother, and he knew that's exactly what was coming.

"Wait a minute now," his mother called out, grabbing him by the back pocket of his Wranglers as he turned to leave the kitchen. "What's going on with the two of you?"

He wanted to tell his mother it was nothing to worry about, that things were going great between them, but he knew without a doubt it was the complete opposite. It would be a straight-up lie for him to tell his mother things were going good when they truly weren't.

"I know something isn't right because she called and told me that she wouldn't be out for a while," his mother stated matter-of-factly. "And she put an end to the riding lessons for Allie, too. Or at least, until further notice."

Drew already knew all of that. Missing Becca was one thing, but not seeing Allie and having her attend riding lessons... That hit him square in the chest. Maybe his brothers were right about him... Maybe he was getting soft.

"Is there anything you want to talk about?" his mother asked, patting a vacant chair next to her as she took a seat at the kitchen table. "I know you're a grown man and more than capable of handling your own, but we all need advice on love from time to time."

He let out a slight chuckle but quickly righted himself when he realized his mother wasn't joking. She was serious, and she was expecting him to be as well.

"There's really nothing more I can do, Ma," he said. "She's asked for time and space, and I've been giving her all the time and space she needs while I'm left hoping and praying she doesn't leave me hanging."

His mother slowly nodded, silently acknowledging his fears. He had never been one to fear anything, at least not until Becca and Allie came into his life.

"What are you going to do once that arm of yours is fully healed up and the rodeo starts calling your name again?" his mother asked, a furrowed expression on her face. He knew what she was thinking.

How could he make Becca hurry up and choose when he didn't even know what he was planning to do? "I think it's best for you to take however long she's taken and decide what it is you truly want. Because girls like her don't come around you ranch boys all that often, and I'm here to tell you that Becca and her little girl are one of a kind."

He nodded, knowing his mother was right. He needed to figure out if he was completely ready to give up bull riding and rodeo competitions in order to settle down. He couldn't help but wonder if settling down was something Becca was interested in doing with him, but he knew only time would tell.

CHAPTER TWENTY-SIX

Becca rounded up Allie and Rosie into the backseat of her car before heading to the ranch. She carried the gallon of ice cream she'd grabbed the night before at the store to the front of the car and placed it in the passenger seat as she turned the key in the ignition.

Allie didn't have a clue as to where they were headed, as Becca had just mentioned ice cream at the park. Thankfully, that had been enough to pause the questions for now.

Or at least until they passed the county park and headed out onto the oh-so-familiar back roads leading to the Dixon Ranch. She smiled in the rearview mirror as Allie and Rosie sang along to a song on the radio.

She guided the car around the last turn in the

small town and drove onto the blacktop of the county highway. The jaunt between Becca's mother's house and the Dixon Ranch didn't take longer than ten minutes, but today it might have taken less time because Becca was in a hurry to get the ice cream inside before it melted all over the inside of her car. She supposed seeing Drew had something to do with the pressure she'd placed on the accelerator, too.

"Mama, where are we going?" Allie called from the backseat, spinning around and looking behind them as they headed away from the coziness of their small town and toward the wide-open spaces of Montana.

"Somewhere special, baby," Becca said, smiling back at her daughter with a renewed energy and confidence to go after what she wanted in life. She had everything she ever wanted right there in the backseat of her car—a spitting image of herself at six years old smiling back at her. But now Becca had one more thing to add to the list, and she was on her way to tell him that she was done wasting time.

"Mama," Allie shrieked from the backseat as Becca pulled the car into the driveway leading them to the main house. There was something comforting about arriving at the ranch-style house with several miles of land and pastures surrounding it, not to mention the small cabins scattered throughout the property for the Dixon brothers and the extra ranch hands they'd hired.

"We're here, Rosie," Allie informed her best friend. Allie's eyes filled with tears of happiness as she pointed out her favorite animals at the ranch. Becca shifted the car into park, and it didn't take long before Allie was tugging Rosie out of the car. Rosie tagged along with a bright smile on her face. "Let's go. I'll introduce you. But first, they have a tire swing."

Becca watched as the girls scrambled off toward the old tree on the north side of the property. She waited a minute to make sure they'd get along and share the swing without bickering before grabbing the gallon of ice cream and carrying it up the steps.

She hesitated a minute, shading her eyes from the mid-day sun and looking around for any sign of Drew. No sooner had she turned back to the door than she was greeted by the one and only Drew Dixon.

"Hey," she said, the word barely managing to leave her lips as she stared up at him. He looked down at her, focusing on her eyes as she stared into his.

"Bec," he said, swiping a hand through his hair and giving her a once-over. She felt the heat creep into her cheeks as she tried to turn away and hide it. "What are you doing here?"

She felt foolish for having thought he'd be excited

to see her. She should have known better than to think he'd want anything to do with her now.

"I mean," he said, "I'm happy to see you. It's just... I didn't think... I wasn't expecting—"

"I brought ice cream."

She held it up and laughed at how ridiculous it sounded as soon as she'd said it.

"A peace offering?" he asked with a low grunt.

She offered a subtle shrug and said, "Something like that."

"I have to say I wasn't quite expecting that either," he said with a grin before pulling her in close to him. She looked up at him as he leaned in. Closing the distance between them with just a tilt of his head, he kissed her. His lips pressed firmly against hers as he held her tightly against his chest. She'd be a fool not to admit how much she'd missed him.

"I've missed you," she said, placing her hands on his face as she stared up at him. His eyes were filled with a flurry of mixed emotions, and she could only imagine what was going through his mind.

"I've missed you more," he said, kissing her once again and laughing when Allie and Rosie caught them. Turning, he scooped Allie up beside him. Becca watched the loving exchange shared between them as she waited for Allie to introduce Drew to Rosie. It didn't take long for Drew to offer a hand out to Rosie as he said, "It's nice to meet you."

A fit of laughter ensued at Drew's antics, and Allie excitedly pointed out the ice cream Becca had planned on getting inside before it melted.

Becca held it up and said, "I suppose I better get this inside before it melts?"

Drew took a hold of the handle and set it off to the side. "There's plenty of time to worry about melting ice cream," he said, tracing his thumb along her jawline and tucking that one strand of hair behind her ear as he smiled. "Right now, I want to talk about me and you."

Becca smiled up at him and said, "Thank you for giving me time to figure things out. I'm sorry that I pushed you away. It's been a rollercoaster—"

"Tell me about it," Drew teased.

"I like what we have, and I don't want it to end," Becca said, leaning into Drew as he wrapped his arm around her and held her close. "Just as long as we can take things slowly, I think everything will be okay."

Drew stepped back and looked her in the eyes. "I promise that we've got nothing but time. Beating eight seconds is a thing of the past."

Becca's heart stopped beating at the mention of Drew giving up the rodeo. "I can't ask you to give up the one thing you love the most, Drew."

"You don't have to ask me," Drew said, offering her that one-of-a-kind, dimple-filled smile of his, and her heart missed a few beats as the butterflies fluttered to life again in the pit of her stomach. She caught her breath and righted herself in front of him, willing her heart to stop beating so hard against her chest. "I've done a lot of thinking lately, and I'm pretty sure it's time to give it up and focus on what matters the most to me."

Becca stared at him with uncertainty. Her thoughts were all over the place. There was no way she would expect him to give up the rodeo. Not something he'd enjoyed forever.

"Becca, listen to me," Drew said, placing his hand on the side of her face and refocusing her attention. "When you asked me for time and a little extra space, I gave it to you," he continued once she nodded, "but I also gave myself some time to think about what it is I truly want in life."

Her breath caught in her throat at the realization they both needed time to figure things out, not just her. He continued, "Chasing rodeos and riding bulls might've been something I enjoyed a little too much, to be honest. And ever since you and Allie came into my life, I haven't even thought about beating the clock and winning that eight-second ride."

Becca nodded along with what he was saying. He was sincere with his words, and it comforted her to know she could tell he was speaking from the heart. She could see in his eyes and hear it in his voice.

"To tell you the truth, Bec," he said, tracing his

thumb along her cheek as he stared into her eyes. "I've got everything I'll ever need right here. This ranch, having you in my arms, and Allie playing on the tire swing with a friend... is *home* to me."

She felt more than confident she'd made the right decision on not only coming back to Woodford Creek, but back to Dixon Ranch. When she'd first arrived back in the small town and had moved in with her mother, she'd had doubts about how things were going to turn out for her and Allie. She hadn't expected a handsome cowboy to sweep her off her feet so soon after her divorce from Chad, but there was no denying that's exactly what happened.

"I'll spend all of the time I have left on the clock with you and Allie if that means I'll be happy for the rest of my life," Drew promised, kissing the tip of Becca's nose before glancing over his shoulder at Allie and Rosie. He turned back to Becca, who was still trying to calm the rhythm of her heart, and said, "How about we take the girls inside and have some ice cream? Do you think they'd like that?"

"I think they'd like that a lot," Becca said, smiling up at him and wondering how she'd gotten so lucky to find a man like Drew to care so much about her and Allie. She'd prayed for time to heal her insecurities and for God to guide her along, showing her how to love and trust again. He'd answered her prayers by putting Drew Dixon into her life.

Thanks to the cowboy staring back at her now, while holding her close to him and promising her a future of happiness and a feeling of home, Becca knew deep down she'd be okay, and so would Allie.

All because two people decided to come back home, to the small town of Woodford Creek, everything was going to be okay.

Without having gone through what Chad had put her through, she would have never come back home. The chance of connecting with Drew Dixon hadn't seemed like such a blessing at first. She'd thought he was like all the other cowboys she'd known at one time or another. But now, with Drew standing by her side in his mother's kitchen, scooping ice cream into bowls for the girls, she realized she'd been completely wrong about him.

Allie wrapped her arms around both of their legs, securing them tightly with a bear hug as she said, "This is the best night ever."

"I agree, Allie-gator," Drew said, shooting a wink at Becca. At the sound of tiny snickers by their feet, Becca silently shook her head. The game her mother had made between her and Allie had become something for Drew to share with Becca's little girl, too.

She didn't think her heart could stand to skip any more beats, but there it was, every time Drew shot her that look with his dimpled grin and soft brown eyes staring back at her.

"Does this mean we're moving to the ranch now?" Allie asked, climbing up to the counter next to them with her bowl of ice cream. She slid a few things out of the way and made room for Rosie to join in on the fun of asking questions.

Becca looked at Drew then back at Allie. Before she had a chance to explain, Drew said, "Hopefully sooner rather than later, but for right now, we're just going to enjoy one another's company. Which means you're more than welcome to be at the ranch anytime."

Drew shot a look at Becca, and she nodded with a smile. He'd done fairly well with handling Allie's question, she'd give him that.

"As long as your mother says it's okay," he quickly added, leaning in for one last kiss before digging into his own bowl full of ice cream.

Becca thanked God for answered prayers and the path he'd given them both on their way back home. Standing next to Drew, she felt the familiarity of what home was supposed to feel like. They had each been down a tough road, but they'd eventually found their way back home. And home was right where they belonged.

EPILOGUE

"Are you sure about this?"

Drew heard the hesitation in Becca's voice the minute she asked the question. She followed closely behind, mirroring him and Allie step for step as they made their way to the stables.

"I've never been so sure about anything else in my life," Drew stated matter-of-factly, catching an excited giggle from Allie.

Drew had spent the better half of the last couple of months working with Chance and getting him broken and used to riding. He'd set a goal to have the horse broken and ready to ride by early fall, and from the looks of it, they were right on time.

Drew shoved the stable door open and motioned for his girls to go on ahead of him. It hadn't taken Becca too long to warm up to Simon, and with Allie's encouragement and light coaching, she'd climbed into the saddle and had forgotten all of her reasons for not trusting horses.

Drew smiled as he reached out for Becca's hand before leading her to Simon's stall.

"You and Allie want to take Simon while I saddle up and ready Chance? It'll only take me a few minutes," Drew said, patting Simon while waiting for Becca to go along with it. She didn't have time to agree or disagree before Allie answered for her and made her way into Simon's stall.

Drew shot a wink at Allie and grinned. The two of them had planned on a day like today, praying that not only Chance, but Becca too, would be ready to ride.

"Are you sure he's ready?" Becca asked, climbing into the saddle behind Allie. Drew stood next to Simon, holding him steady as his girls positioned themselves in the saddle. It'd taken Becca a few rides with Drew to warm up to Simon and to trust him. Allie had made the comment about wanting her mother to ride with her a few times at dinner a couple of weeks ago while they all sat around the dining room table at the main house with the rest of the Dixon bunch. Becca couldn't promise her little girl that she'd ever be ready to ride, but she had promised to give it her best shot.

And even though it had taken Becca a lot longer

than either of them expected, she was keeping her promise to Allie.

Drew looked up at Allie before stepping away from Simon, wanting to make sure she was good to go. The smile on Allie's face told him everything he needed to know as he left his two favorite girls atop his best horse before making his way over to Chance's stall.

If someone would have told him there was life outside of the rodeo circuit, he wouldn't have believed them. He'd been too focused on the competition and caught up in beating the clock to realize that there were more important things waiting for him.

He stepped into Chance's stall, taking it nice and easy before saddling him. He shot a glance at Allie and Becca and smiled when Becca's eyes met his.

A part of him knew deep down that he never planned on falling in love and sticking around. And the good Lord knew he wouldn't have if it hadn't been for Becca and Allie. If he were to be honest, he believed the good Lord brought him back home and placed them in his life—giving him a reason to settle down and to finally find a place to call home.

"Let's do this," Drew said, confidently mirroring Allie's excitement with a tip of his hat as he led Chance to the wide open pasture. He nodded his approval as Allie guided Simon right alongside Chance.

"I never thought we'd see the day," Drew said with a smile. "But here we are, Al. We've managed to get Bec in a saddle and a saddle on Chance."

Allie's face lit up with a smile, and Drew felt a slight tug in his heart. There was something about her that had Drew all in. To be honest, she'd won his heart over the very first day they'd met.

There wasn't anything he wouldn't do for that little girl, and the same could be said for her mother as well.

"What do you say we show your mom one of our favorite spots by the creek?"

Allie's face beamed with a smile as she adjusted the cowgirl hat Drew had given her the day she'd graduated from her riding lessons. "Did you remember to bring what you said you were going to bring?"

Drew nodded with a smile as he discreetly patted the front pocket of his flannel shirt. Becca raised a brow of suspicion but he cheesily dismissed it with a wink before setting off in the direction of the creek.

The moment Drew's feet hit the ground, he knew there was no turning back. It was now or never, and there was no better time than now.

He patiently waited for Allie and Becca to climb down from the saddle. He'd thought about this moment time and again, hoping he'd get it right and wouldn't be too nervous.

He'd spent half his life gripping the ropes of fate while riding a two-thousand-pound bull and had never once been as nervous as he was at this very moment.

Allie pulled on her mother's hand, bringing her over to Drew and pushing them closer together. "Go ahead, Drew, ask her," Allie said, adjusting her hat once again as she looked up at the two of them.

"Ask me what?" Becca asked, looking from Allie back to Drew. Drew's heart raced, beating hard inside of his chest as he stared Becca in the eye. He cleared his throat as he took a step forward, closing the distance between them. Becca stood frozen in front of him, no doubt trying to figure out what this was all about. He offered her a reassuring smile as he reached into his pocket.

"Becca," he said, trying like crazy to slow his pounding heart long enough to get his words straight. The last thing he wanted to do was make a fool of himself. "There's a lot of things I'm not too sure of when it comes to this life of mine…"

His words trailed off as he looked down at Allie, who was now holding tightly to a bouquet of wildflowers with a bright smile on her face. She nodded, encouraging him to keep going as she looked from him to Becca.

Becca's eyes left his for a split second, and he knew she had the pieces together no sooner than she accepted her daughter's flowers.

"But one thing I'm most definitely certain about is how much I love you and Allie. There's no doubt in my mind that I want the two of you in my life for as long as I live," he said, removing the small black box from his pocket and dropping to one knee. He fumbled with it for a minute, but Allie stepped in and assisted him with opening it. "Thanks, kiddo."

He righted himself and looked up at Becca, who was now standing in front of him with a trembling hand covering her mouth and tears in her eyes.

"There isn't anything I wouldn't do for either of you, Bec," he said, looking down at the ring glistening in the late afternoon sunlight. "I know we talked about taking things slow and moving one day at a time… and we can still do that, but I wanted to make sure you knew just how serious I am about spending the rest of my life with you. I love you, Bec."

Becca wiped a stray tear from her face as he stared up at her, waiting for the right moment to continue with his mission. "And I love you, too, Drew." She looked at Allie and back at him. "*We both love you.*"

Drew smiled with a nod, taking a moment to clear the emotion settling in as he cleared his throat before he asked, "Becca, will you marry me?"

Becca nodded, trying her best to keep the tears at

bay as Allie jumped up and down and shouted, "Yes, she says yes!"

Drew fumbled with the ring before carefully sliding it onto Becca's finger. There had been a moment in time when he'd thought she'd say no, but not right now. Standing there in front of her, he had no doubts about what the future might hold for the three of them right there in Woodford Creek—a place he could now call *home* and mean it.

Drew carefully stood up before wrapping his arm around Becca. He slid his cowboy hat off and placed it on top of Becca's head before pulling her in close and meeting her lips with his in the wide-open space of the Dixon Ranch in the heart of Montana.

Did you enjoy what you've read? Do you want to stay up-to-date with new releases and sales?
Sign Up for Christina's Newsletter Here:
https://www.subscribepage.com/authorcbutrum

A NOTE FROM THE AUTHOR

If you enjoyed *The Cowboy's Home*, please consider leaving a review.

Thank you!

Continue reading the Dixon Ranch Series today!
The Cowboy's Heart

ABOUT THE AUTHOR

Christina Butrum launched her writing career in 2015 with the release of The Fairshore Series.

Writing contemporary fiction, she brings realistic situations with swoon-worthy romance to the pages - allowing her readers to fall in love right along with the characters.

When she isn't busy writing, Christina enjoys spending time with her family. Christina Butrum looks forward to publishing many more books for her readers to enjoy.

www.authorchristinabutrum.com

Sign Up for Christina's Newsletter Here:

https://www.subscribepage.com/authorcbutrum
Join Christina's Group Here:
https://www.facebook.com/groups/
ButrumsBookBabes

- facebook.com/authorcbutrum
- twitter.com/authorcbutrum
- amazon.com/author/christinabutrum
- bookbub.com/profile/christina-butrum

ALSO BY CHRISTINA BUTRUM

FAIRSHORE SERIES

Second Chances

Unexpected Chances

Fair Chances

KATE'S DUET

Kate's Valentine

Kate's Forever

CEDAR VALLEY SERIES

All She Ever Wanted

Everything She Needed

All She Ever Desired

A MAPLE GLEN ROMANCE SERIES

It Takes Two

Coffee for Two

RSVP for Two

Room for Two

Lesson for Two

One plus Two

Christmas for Two

DIXON RANCH SERIES
The Cowboy's Home
The Cowboy's Heart
The Cowboy's Hope

THE COWBOYS OF PINE CREEK
A Pine Creek Homecoming - *Coming Soon!*
A Pine Creek Second Chance - *Coming Soon!*
A Pine Creek Summer - *Coming Soon!*
A Pine Creek Christmas Miracle - *Coming Soon!*
A Pine Creek Wedding - *Coming Soon!*
A Pine Creek Holiday - *Coming Soon!*

STANDALONE NOVELS
No Place Like Home - Love in Seattle
Saving Jenna

INTERCONNECTED NOVELLA
Sweet on Love - A Lover's Landing Novella
Starting Over in Silver Leaf Falls - A Silver Leaf Falls Novella
Falling for the Single Dad - Hopeless Romantics of Willow Ridge - Book 6

SWEET PROMISE PRESS NOVELS

Choosing Chelsea - A Gold Coast Retrievers Novel

No Time for Goodbyes - A No Brides Club Novel

No Time for Mistletoe - A No Brides Club Novel

Never miss a new release!

Sign up for Christina Butrum's newsletter:

https://www.subscribepage.com/authorcbutrum

Made in United States
North Haven, CT
25 November 2024